OZETTE'S
DESTINY

D0167295

TALES FROM FARLANDIA

BOOK ONE

OZETTE'S DESTINY

JUDY PIERCE

Pants On Fire Press
Winter Garden Toronto London
Madrid São Paulo New Delhi Tokyo

Pants On Fire Press, Winter Garden 34787

Text copyright © 2013 by Judy Pierce

All rights reserved. No part of this book may be transmitted or reproduced in any form by any means without written permission from the publisher, Pants On Fire Press. For information contact Pants On Fire Press.

All names, places, incidents, and characters in this book are fictitious, and any resemblance to actual persons, living or dead, is purely coincidental.

Visit us at www.PantsOnFirePress.com

Illustrations and art copyright © 2013 by Pants On Fire Press

Art by Natalia Nesterova
Book design by David M. F. Powers

The publisher is not responsible for recipes or websites (or their content).

First edition: 2013

Printed in the United States of America

Library of Congress Cataloging-in-Publication data

Pierce, Judy.

Ozette's destiny / Judy Pierce. – 1st ed.

p. cm.

ISBN 978-0-9827271-9-5

Series : Tales from Farlandia.

Summary : Ozette, a rare white squirrel, must flee Our World when she is blamed for the destruction of the forest, simply because she is different.

[1. Squirrels --Fiction. 2. Animals --Fiction. 3. Friendship --Fiction. 4. Magic --Fiction. 5. Fantasy --Fiction.] I. Title. II. Series.

PZ7.P6144 Oz 2013

[Fic] --dc23   2012918023

This book is dedicated to The Divine Miss Piddlewinks, the squirrel who started me on this amazing journey.

Judy Pierce's wonderful white squirrel, Ozette, represents white squirrels everywhere but more than that, she lives in a magical world inhabited by fairies, elves, animals who talk, and sheer enchantment. This book appeals to children of all ages, including those who haven't seen a real child in decades. Come and lose yourself in Pierce's Farlandia. You'll relish the trip.

Darlene Arden
Certified Animal Behavior Consultant
Author, *The Complete Cat's Meow, Small Dogs, Big Hearts, Rover Get Off Her Leg!*

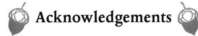 Acknowledgements

This book would not exist without the encouragement and support of the many **friends** who loved reading the Ozette stories online. You are the best! Thanks to my **children**, especially my daughter, **Gail**, who insisted that I write the book and to my grandson, **Madison**, who sat in the back seat of our Subaru while I read the manuscript all the way from Tennessee to North Carolina. Thanks to Author **Darlene Arden** for her encouragement and for loaning me her fairy friend, Ariel, the impish fairy in this book. Many thanks to friend and editor **DanaRae Pomeroy** who offered wonderful counsel as I fleshed out the story. Big thanks to fellow author **Julie Casey** who designed my web page. My thanks to the wildlife rehabilitators who taught me so much about the bond between humans and squirrels. I am grateful to the squirrels and Bichons who have shared our lives, teaching and enriching us, especially one very special white squirrel named **Ozette**. Thanks to the wonderful folks at Pants on Fire Press who made me feel such a part of their team – **Becca**, my editor, **Cris**, from marketing, **Natalia**, who designed the beautiful artwork and **David**, my publisher. You are great! A huge thank you to my wonderful husband, **Jim**, who encouraged my "overactive imagination" and who supported me every step of the way.

Chapter One

A Scruffy Nest Guest

If you're lucky enough to slip through the thin veil that separates Earth World from the magical kingdoms, you might encounter Farland, a vast territory of lakes, babbling streams, rolling meadows, mountains and gentle forests ruled by Queen Beatrix. It's an enchanting land filled with fairies, elves, a wise and kind princess and animals living extraordinary lives. It's also a land of unexplored adventures and magical moments.

And if you venture to the far western corner of Farland, you'll find the most exquisite jewel in the territory: an old-growth forest called Farlandia, a lush woodland rich with giant hardwoods, ever-greens, fern groves and flowing streams lined with lush moss banks.

And if you look high up to the top of the tallest ancient maple tree, you will find a unique squirrel named Ozette. When she first arrived, no one in the forest had ever seen a squirrel like her, for her coat was a bright white, except for a small splash of gray on her forehead and a hint of pale gray down the center of her back.

Ozette had appeared in Farlandia three full-moon cycles ago during the mild winter and claimed the stately maple tree for her home. Although shy at first, she quickly became a favorite among the fairies, elves and other woodland creatures because of her kindness, loyalty and fun-loving nature.

She was a gracious and generous hostess, and it wasn't unusual to see friends gathering under her tree to sip tea and chat before their afternoon naps. Though most of the time she chattered away happily and fussed over her friends, she sometimes had a sad, faraway look in her dark eyes when she thought no one was looking. But her friends were reluctant to pry into Ozette's past, thinking it may be impolite, so they never asked too many questions.

Milligan Mouse, who could never keep his mouth shut, once asked Ozette if she was born in some exotic tree that bore glistening white nuts.

"Could that be why you're a white squirrel?" he asked, his dark eyes bright with curiosity.

Ozette had simply smiled and passed around a plate of walnut-encrusted jumbledberry scones.

Once, a fairy mistakenly referred to her coloration as albino and Ozette gently shook her head. She related to all creatures that were different, and she certainly admired the beauty of the unusual albino foxes, bears and other albino creatures. But she also didn't want, or need, to pretend to be someone she was not.

One spring afternoon, when the ice had disappeared from the forest ponds and succulent buds were swelling on the trees, Ozette lay stretched out full-length on her tree limb. Her back legs dangled down either side of the limb and her chin rested on her front paws. She was just dozing off after playing a rousing game of "kick the acorn" with her fairy friends when she heard a soft whine. She first ignored the sound, thinking she was dreaming. When she heard it again, louder this time, she peered sleepily over the side of the branch. Her eyes sprang wide open when she saw a scruffy white creature sitting under her tree, looking forlorn and confused. She crept cautiously down her tree to get a better look.

The creature looked a little like the beautiful dog Cassady who often accompanied the queen's sister, Princess Abrianna. Like Cassady, this creature had four legs, two ears and a tail...but was much, much smaller. And much, much dirtier. While the princess' dog was a silky, shiny golden retriever, this little creature was small and white – well, mostly white.

There were several dirty places on its rump, where it had apparently sat in some mud. It had a very black nose, dark button eyes, long floppy ears and a snowy plumed tail that curled over its back, similar to Ozette's own majestic tail.

"Excuse me," Ozette said timidly as she poked her head around the tree trunk, ready to make a hasty retreat if the creature proved hostile. "Who are you?"

The creature looked startled and craned its neck to see who was speaking.

"Oh hello," it said, walking over to the tree. Noting Ozette's hesitancy, it assured her. "Don't worry. I won't chase you. Chasing little animals is how I got myself into this mess in the first place."

"Um, exactly *what* kind of animal are you?" Ozette asked.

The creature drew itself up to its full height, which wasn't more than ten inches, but still well over twice as tall as Ozette.

"I am a royal canine. In fact, I'm Queen Beatrix's beloved companion. My name is Duchess Zorina Muffaroonie, but my queen calls me Duchess Zorina," she said proudly. "I am a Bichon Frise, a dog of royalty."

Then the little dog's bravado failed and her head dropped low. Looking plaintively at Ozette, she whimpered, "and I'm lost, very lost."

Lost? How could anyone get lost in these woods? You just had to follow your animal instincts, Ozette thought, but didn't say out loud because she didn't want to hurt the little dog's feelings.

"My name is Ozette and I live here," she introduced herself. "How ever did you end up in the forest?"

The dog sat at the base of the tree and looked up at Ozette.

"I'm never allowed outside the palace alone. I'm a house pet, you see, but I've always wanted to see the outside world. When the cook left the back door open for a minute, I saw my chance and ran out into the backyard. Then I saw a rabbit bounding down the lawn and I couldn't stop myself from running after it."

Seeing the sudden look of horror on the squirrel's face, Duchess Zorina quickly added, "but it was just for fun. I would never ever hurt a rabbit, or any other creature."

"Then what happened?" Ozette asked.

The dog whimpered again. "I fell into a river and the strong current carried me far away from my queen. When the water finally calmed down, I was able to scramble onto shore. I've spent three nights in these woods," she said, shivering. "I'm cold and hungry, and I want to go home. If I ever get back to the royal castle, I'll never leave my queen's lap again."

Ozette thought for a minute and took pity on the miserable little creature. "It's supposed to be drizzly and cold this evening. You'll need warm shelter and food. There's room in my nesting hole for both of us. I don't suppose you can climb a tree?" she asked hopefully.

"I'm a dog, not a monkey!" Duchess Zorina squeaked. "I'm accustomed to sleeping on a lavender satin pillow, not scrambling up tree trunks. Oh, what am I to do?" the little dog asked anxiously as she paced beneath the tree.

"How to get you up the tree…hmm…" Ozette pondered, tapping her paw on her chin. Her brain may have only been the size of a walnut, but it was fast and creative. Suddenly she motioned for the dog to stay there and scampered up her tree.

"GWACK! GWACK! GWACK!" she shouted, her tail flagging wildly as she explained her dilemma to whatever forest friends were listening.

Duchess Zorina put her paws over her ears at the shrill sound.

Within seconds, there came an answering "GWACK! GWACK!" After several more "GWACK GWACKS" and a couple of "TWARK TWARKS," five husky gray squirrels came bounding through the treetops to Ozette's tree.

They stopped short when they saw the little white dog.

"*This* is what you need our help with…a *dog*?!" Guido, the biggest gray, asked, as he glared suspiciously. "It won't chase us, will it?"

"I'm not an *it*," Duchess Zorina said. "I'm a *she*, and a *royal she* at that. I don't chase squirrels," she said, then muttered under her breath, "unless they call me names, of course."

"You know who could help?" said another muscular male named Rowdy. "Princess Abrianna.

We could take the mutt over to her cottage. She's the queen's sister and will know what to do, especially since it thinks it's royalty."

"Mutt! Did you call me a mutt?" Duchess Zorina squeaked indignantly.

"Mutt, dog, whatever," Guido said shrugging and turning back to the group. "I saw Princess Abrianna yesterday, camping near Moonlight Creek. But I don't know when she'll return to her cottage in Farlandia."

The other males were quiet, assessing the situation.

"Come on, guys. Have some sympathy for our poor guest," Ozette pleaded. "She's cold, hungry, tired and needs our help. We need to hoist her up into my nest so she can have something to eat and sleep here tonight. Then I'll need you to come back tomorrow morning to help carry her down the tree. And *then* I'll try to get her home. Someway. Somehow. One problem at a time."

"Well, Ozette, our first problem is that nesting hole of yours isn't big enough for her to fit through," said Rowdy, eying the plump dog compared to the little round nesting hole.

Ozette hurried up her tree and, using her razor-sharp teeth, enlarged the hole until it was just big enough for the little dog to fit through, she hoped. She could repair it later.

"Done!" she said efficiently.

The squirrels gathered around the dog, Grady and Rowdy pulling from the front and the other squirrels, Grayson, Dooley and Guido, pushing from the back. Slowly, they began tugging the white dog up the tall maple tree.

"How can such a little puffball weigh so much?" Rowdy said, tugging at the dog.

"I am not overweight, I am just really fluffy," Duchess Zorina protested, her dark eyes filling with tears.

Ozette put her paws on her ample hips. "That was very unkind, Rowdy. I expect better from my squirrel friends."

Rowdy hung his head and mumbled a contrite, "Sorry."

"Look, guys. She's been outside on her own for three nights. Quit with the insults and just help me."

Push. Grunt. Shove. It was slow work, but they finally pushed and pulled the exhausted dog up the tree and into Ozette's nest.

As the big gray squirrels stood huffing and puffing, Ozette thanked them kindly and said she'd see them in the morning when they came back to carry the dog down. All the squirrels groaned in unison.

"I don't know, Ozette," Grayson, the smallest of the squirrels, said worriedly as they exited the nesting hole. "Getting her down will be much harder than hoisting her up. And what if we drop her? It's a long way to the ground."

The little dog shuddered. Ozette patted her soft, fluffy head.

"Don't worry, Duchess Zorina. I'll think of something. Remember, we're solving one problem at a time."

After the gray squirrels left, Ozette began searching through her stash of food to find dinner for her unexpected guest.

"Our cook usually fixes me a nice juicy steak," Duchess Zorina suggested hopefully.

Ozette shook her head in disbelief. Clearly she was not cooking a steak inside her nest. Instead she offered her guest some homemade pecan snookeroons and a jumbledberry scone. The little dog ate hungrily then curled up amidst the leaves, feathers and mosses that blanketed Ozette's cozy nest.

"Thank you for being so kind to me," she said sleepily. "I don't mean to be such a bother. It's just that I'm not used to this outdoor woodsy stuff and I'm scared."

Ozette patted the dog gently on her back. "I'll get you home. Somehow."

And then Ozette did something she never thought she would do, as it wasn't every day that she had a dog sharing her nest. The two-pound squirrel cuddled up next to a ten-pound dog and fell sound asleep, only to be awakened several times by Duchess Zorina running in her sleep and yipping softly during a dog-dream. Ozette gently rested her paw on the dog's nose to calm her, and the two fell back into quiet slumber.

Chapter Two
WHAT GOES UP, MUST COME DOWN

Ozette was awakened early by Duchess Zorina's stirring. The little dog was looking anxiously out the hole down to the ground below.

"Ozette, thank you for letting me sleep up here. I feel so safe with you, but I'm really scared to have those squirrels trying to get me down this tree. What if I fall? I don't think they like me very much, anyway."

"They just don't quite know what to make of

you," Ozette said. "But I may have an idea to get you down this tree that doesn't involve pushing and pulling."

Ozette gave Duchess Zorina some leftover walnut banana bread and climbed out onto her limb. "BWACK! BWACK!" she called, this time for another group of special friends.

A few minutes later, Ozette's fairy friends Ariel, Sydney and Annika came flitting over, their gossamer wings shining in the morning sun. They were followed by Oliver, Ozette's dearest elf friend, who flew close behind and performed a spectacular array of intricate flips and dips before landing on Ozette's tree.

After explaining her dilemma, Ozette told her winged pals her new plan to bring the dog back down to the ground.

"Whoa," Ariel exclaimed, her violet eyes wide. "That will take a whole flock of us."

Oliver cupped his chin in his hands. His pointed ears were twitching, a sure sign he was thinking.

"I think we can do it," he said confidently. "Just give me a few minutes to gather the forces."

Off he flew while the fairies flitted into Ozette's nest to meet the new visitor. Duchess Zorina had never seen a fairy before, since most of them typically stayed in the far reaches of the woodlands, which were nowhere near the palace. Fascinated by the diminutive creatures, she sniffed Ariel's glossy black curls and pointed ears. Annika offered the dog her delicate hand, and Duchess Zorina held up her own paw to shake. Sydney giggled as Duchess Zorina licked the fairy's nut-brown face with an affectionate dog kiss.

While the group dined on honeysuckle tea and nutty fruitinas, Ozette told Duchess Zorina her new plan and the dog's mouth dropped wide open.

"You think that will work?" she asked.

Ozette nodded confidently. She didn't want the dog to know that this was their only good option since the burley squirrels were so doubtful they could carry her safely down the tree.

Suddenly they heard a loud whirring noise. Ozette stuck her head out of the tree and beheld the most awesome sight: Hundreds of fairies and elves were flying in a "V" formation toward her nest.

"They're here!" she shouted, clapping her paws. "Come, Duchess Zorina. Climb out on the thickest part of this limb. The fairies and elves will fly you down to the ground."

Frightened at the commotion, poor Duchess

Zorina scurried to the farthest corner of Ozette's nest, hid her head in a pile of leaves and started shaking. Ozette went over to the little dog and stroked her rump.

"I'll be with you. Fairies and elves are stronger than they look. It will be fine," Ozette assured her. She coaxed the frightened dog onto the limb, while the fairies and elves took hold of her gently with their tiny hands.

"OK," Sydney commanded. "At the count of three – One. Two. Three. Liftoff!"

What a sight! The dog was literally covered with brightly colored fairies and elves who carefully lifted her into the air and slowly, ever-so-slowly, lowered her to the ground in a blaze of brilliant color. They set the dog down gently then hovered over her reassuringly, while Ozette raced down the tree and jumped around with joy!

Duchess Zorina was so relieved; she started running in ever-widening circles, as fast as her stubby legs would carry her! She yipped happily and returned to Ozette.

"Thank you all so much! That was *most* exciting!

"Now I just need to get home to my queen," she said excitedly, and looked at Ozette expectantly.

"Who knows where Queen Beatrix's palace

is?" Ozette asked the assembled elves and fairies.

"It's that way," said Oliver, twitching his elfin ears and pointing confidently due east.

"No it isn't. It's over there," said Sydney, gesturing northwest.

"You're both wrong," insisted Ariel. "It's over there." She pointed south.

While the little creatures argued among themselves, their tiny voices creating a noisy buzz, Ozette and Duchess Zorina sat under a shady hemlock tree.

"I've never been to the queen's palace," Ozette said to the dog. "What other creatures who live in the forest might know the way?"

Duchess Zorina was silent for several minutes, and then her eyes lit up. "Do you have any unicorns around here? They visit our vegetable gardens at the palace. If we could find one, maybe it could tell us the way."

"What a great idea," Ozette said. "Hmm. I know! Princess Abrianna often has unicorns in her vegetable garden. She's not home now, but let's head over and see if any are there this morning."

Chapter Three

Flying High - Maxwell
To The Rescue

Down the tree-lined path they went, dog and squirrel.

"My friends call me DZ," said the dog. "You could call me that."

Ozette nodded and smiled.

DZ regaled Ozette with stories from the palace – grand balls, feasts that made Ozette's mouth water and silly antics of the humans who lived there. Ozette chuckled, and soon it seemed like the duo had been friends forever.

They finally came to Princess Abrianna's home. Ozette sighed. Princess Abrianna's cottage almost made her want to be a human. It was charming with its bay windows, stone fireplaces and inviting benches set amid a profusion of flowers and herbs. In one corner of her wildflower garden was a creek that flowed into a clear, inviting pool. It was a favorite cooling-off spot for all the creatures on hot summer days.

Princess Abrianna had a wonderful vegetable garden that Ozette often scavenged – with permission, of course. If she overindulged, the princess would fix her a cup of chamomile or peppermint tea with herbs from her garden, and they would sit in the gazebo near a pond filled with fish and turtles.

It was rumored that Princess Abrianna not only knew the secrets of healing herbs, but could also slip effortlessly from Farlandia into other worlds, although why anyone would want to leave Farlandia was a mystery to Ozette.

They peeked into the garden, but no unicorns were feeding. As they sat silently waiting, DZ's stomach began rumbling.

"Hmm," said Ozette. "We may need another plan if the unicorns don't arrive. But for now, let's take care of that belly!" She led DZ around back, where she knew the princess kept her dog Cassady's dishes.

"Yes!" Ozette shouted, pumping a paw in the air. One dish was full of water, and the other held several home-baked dog cookies.

"I don't know, Ozette. I was taught to not take what belongs to others," DZ said, gazing longingly at the food.

"Princess Abrianna and Cassady will understand," Ozette said, pushing the dish closer to DZ. "They would never want an animal to go hungry. Go ahead."

The dog had just finished gobbling the cookies and slurping the water, when they heard a "wushhh wuuuussh" coming from the sky. They looked up and saw a majestic black unicorn just as it landed gracefully in the garden.

Now, Farland was one of the few magical lands where unicorns were winged, so they knew this beautiful animal came from DZ's home. They ran to the garden, DZ yipping excitedly.

As the two approached, the unicorn looked up from where he was munching lettuce. He looked surprised to see a dog and squirrel running toward him. He stopped eating and cocked his head.

"I know you," he said, looking at DZ. "You're Queen Beatrix's dog. All of Farland has been in an uproar since you disappeared! What happened? Where have you been? Are you safe?" he asked.

DZ told him the story, and the unicorn shook his elegant head in amazement.

"Some silly mice stopped me today with a crazy story about seeing squirrels pushing a little white dog up a tree, but I thought they had overactive imaginations. You know how mice can be."

The dog and squirrel nodded in agreement.

"It was probably Milligan Mouse and his family. He does have a wild imagination, but this time he was right," Ozette said.

The unicorn knelt down with one leg extended and invited the two friends to grab his thick black mane and climb onto his back.

Ozette hesitated. "You take DZ home. I'll head back to my nest," she said.

The unicorn gave a snort. "Nonsense! You're a heroine. You've no idea what a stir this dog's disappearance has caused. The queen will be ecstatic. She will want to meet you and there's even a reward for this little dog's return," he said.

"I just did what was right. I don't need a reward," Ozette replied.

The unicorn dipped his glossy black wing, scooped up Ozette and tossed her onto his back.

"Ever ridden on a unicorn?" he asked.

Ozette shook her head.

"This is your chance. I'm Maxwell, by the way. Off we go!" he shouted, flapping his powerful wings.

And off they flew into the late morning sky, both clinging for dear life to the unicorn, but amazed at the sights beneath them. Farlandia looked so different from high above the trees. Ozette found herself loving the ride. DZ's ears were flapping in the breeze, and she held tightly onto Ozette's paw.

"It's a different world up here, isn't it?" DZ shouted, as if reading her thoughts.

Ozette nodded as she watched meandering streams, flower-studded meadows and verdant forests pass below her, in all their grandeur. She thought she glimpsed lofty mountain peaks in the far distance. She caught her breath at the sheer beauty of it all.

Soon the forest gave way to fields, barns and gardens. Then they came upon the castle itself, a massive gray stone structure topped with three tall bell towers. Ozette's eyes widened as she took in the towering spires and wide balconies.

DZ was bouncing up and down on the unicorn's broad back, almost losing her balance, as Maxwell made a sweeping descent and landed on the lawn in front of the palace. The little dog leaped off of Maxwell's back, barking and yipping. Ozette accompanied her to the front door of the castle, where DZ yipped and barked until it was opened by a stocky young woman carrying a mop and bucket.

"Oh my! Duchess Zorina!" she exclaimed, throwing her hands in the air and dropping the mop and bucket on the marble entryway floor with a splash and a crash.

"And you brought a friend with you! A beautiful white squirrel! Wait until Queen Beatrix sees you're back," she said, scooping up the excited dog and motioning for Ozette to follow them.

"The queen has been in bed, awash in grief, since you disappeared," she said, kissing the top of the dog's head, as she led them into the most opulent bedroom Ozette had ever seen.

Farlandia had much simpler dwellings. The elves, fairies and even Princess Abrianna lived in nice cottages, but nothing like this. The lavish room was decorated with pale yellow and sky blue velvet, satin and silk. Ozette's eyes grew wide, and she couldn't help but compare it to her humble nest.

The queen lay in bed, her eyes red and swollen from crying, and her auburn hair uncombed.

When she caught sight of her beloved companion, Queen Beatrix gasped with joy and held out her arms. DZ flew into them and   smothered the queen's face with wet kisses, washing away tears of happiness.

When DZ had calmed down and was nestled in her lap, the beautiful and very grateful queen turned to Ozette.

"Only an hour ago, we heard a rumor that Maxwell was flying you both here. I hardly dared hope it was true. Please tell me how you found my precious."

Ozette told her the story, and the queen hugged the dog tighter, as she heard how the squirrels had pushed her up a tree, and the fairies and elves had carried her down.

"You know I've offered a generous reward for Duchess Zorina's safe return," the queen said.

Ozette shook her head. "I only wanted to bring her back to you safely," she said, bowing respectfully.

"Most admirable," said the queen, stroking the dog's floppy ears. She asked Ozette to tell her all about Farlandia, as she had never traveled that far into the realm of her own queendom.

Ozette told her about the magnificent old-growth forest, the meadows, the clear streams and rivers, the fields of wild flowers. She spoke of the wildlife, elves and fairies that lived there.

The queen kept nodding her head and saying, "I see."

When Ozette was finished, the queen rang a bell on her bedside table and a woman wearing an apron came scurrying into the room.

"Please fix Ozette and Duchess Zorina lunch, make sure that Maxwell has the choicest vegetables to eat, and summon my top advisors immediately," said the queen, looking thoughtfully at Ozette.

Ozette and DZ dined royally in the cavernous dining room. Ozette was stunned at the size of the table. All of the fairies and elves in Farlandia could dine here and still have room to spare.

At the end of the meal, Ozette and DZ shared a plate of hazelnut tarts filled with raspberry jam.

"I wish you would stay here and live with us," DZ said wistfully to Ozette. "I'll miss you, if you leave."

Ozette had become quite fond of the little puffball and smiled gently. Lifting a fragile china cup in her paws, Ozette explained, "I'll miss you too. But I belong in the woods. I could never be at home here, even though it's so beautiful. But I promise to try to visit."

DZ shuddered. "Yes, you would have to come

here, because I never want to venture into the woods again. I was so lucky to find you," she said, putting her paw over Ozette's.

$\mathcal{C}$hapter $\mathcal{F}$our

$\mathcal{A}$N UN$\mathcal{E}$XP$\mathcal{E}$CT$\mathcal{E}$D R$\mathcal{E}$W$\mathcal{A}$RD

After lunch, DZ showed Ozette around the palace. Ozette was dazzled at the splendid rooms with their intricately carved furniture, brocade draperies and plush carpeting. Ozette giggled as she noted that almost every room held a large portrait of the little dog.

Suddenly, they were summoned into the queen's office. She looked refreshed and her eyes shone happily. She had dressed in a flowing green silk gown, fastened with a braided gold sash. A

26

green ribbon held back her long silky hair. In her hands were some important-looking papers.

"Ozette, I'm eternally grateful to you for bringing my precious Duchess Zorina back home. I have been mulling over what reward to give you. I have many riches, but Farlandia already seems to provide you and your friends with everything you need to be happy."

Ozette nodded in agreement and started to repeat that no reward was necessary, when the queen held up her hand for silence.

"My cousin, Boardmore, and his brother have wanted your section of the woods to build a hunting lodge and to clear land to grow crops."

Ozette shuddered. Hunting! Clearing land! Oh no! She forced her mind back from a dark time in her life and focused on what the queen was saying.

The queen smiled wryly. "Boardmore is not a fan of wilderness unless it suits his own purpose," she said.

"But you have made it sound like such an enchanting place, and I want to reward you and your friends for returning my precious companion. So, this is what I'm doing."

She picked up the papers and showed them to Ozette. "I'm deeding Farlandia to itself, Ozette.

It will be sovereign land, so no one will ever own it and use for their own purposes. And you will be the caretaker of the land, its ruler, much as I rule Farland, to see that it remains in its wild state forever."

Seeing Ozette's shocked and puzzled look, she said firmly, "By belonging to itself, no one can make any claim on it. It will not pass to my heirs, who might not honor my wishes. It's all within the laws of Farland. I'm a good judge of character, and I sense that my trust in you is well founded."

Ozette's mouth dropped open in awe, and she shook her head unbelievingly.

"It's done, Ozette," the queen said firmly, clasping the squirrel's paws in her soft hands to seal the deal.

Ozette's head was spinning. She pondered the queen's gift and felt like she was in a daze.

Maxwell snorted and stomped his giant feet, ready to take to the air. As Ozette headed for the door, DZ raced back into the hall with something in her mouth. She dropped it at Ozette's feet.

"I wanted to give you something of mine. Something to remember me by," she said.

Ozette looked down and gasped. It was a beautiful gold tiara embellished with diamonds, emeralds and rubies. At the peak was a small flower inset with diamonds.

Ozette picked it up with her paw. "Are these real?" she asked.

"Of course they're real," DZ said indignantly. "My queen wouldn't give me fakes. But I want you to have it, Ozette. If you're going to be the caretaker of Farlandia, you need a crown like a real queen."

Ozette started to protest, but DZ gave her the most plaintive look, so she let the dog set it on her head.

"Besides, Ozette, I got it when I was a pup. It fits you much better than it fits me now that I've grown," the dog said.

They hugged tightly, and Ozette slipped out the door and onto Maxwell's back. He flapped his enormous wings, and they were quickly airborne.

Ozette held onto her tiara as Maxwell soared toward the setting sun, the sky laced with violet, salmon and gold. The feeling of awe and freedom was almost overwhelming, and Ozette found herself envying winged creatures. All too soon, Maxwell landed by her tree. She slid off of the unicorn's back onto the ground.

Using his teeth, Maxwell retrieved two intricately woven baskets that had been tied across his flanks.

"These are from the cook. The green one contains nuts for you and your squirrel buddies, and the brown one contains treats for your other friends. Whenever I fly this way again, I'll bring you more. You made quite a hit, Queen Ozette," he said, bowing.

Ozette's head whipped around, and she snorted. "Queen Ozette! What nonsense is that?"

"Well, you have a tiara fit for a queen, and the cook told me Queen Beatrix has deeded Farlandia to itself and appointed you as caretaker. That sounds like the job of a queen to me," he chuckled over his shoulder as he took to the sky.

Ozette shook her head dismissively, stashed the baskets in a bush near her tree and clambered up to her nest. She took off her tiara, hid it in a corner of her nest and went to sleep.

Chapter Five

THE GIFT OF THE ACORN

Ozette awoke as the sun peeked over the horizon, the sky a brilliant canvas of blues streaked with salmons, reds and golds. She loved the early morning hours, when the forest was dew-kissed, and the day held unlimited possibilities.

She sat up, licked her paws, pulled her tail between her legs and began preening herself. When she was satisfied that she looked presentable, she hurried down her maple tree to search for breakfast. Remembering the baskets of goodies from the palace cook, she retrieved the nut-filled basket from the bushes where she had stashed it the night before.

Ozette feasted on the delicious nuts. Some she recognized – walnuts, hazelnuts, hickory nuts and pecans – but others she had never seen. Moon nuts, star nuts, sun nuts, grizzle nuts and chuck nuts. All were tasty, and she decided to save some to plant and grow trees of her own.

Ozette thought back to the lesson that her grandmother, The Divine Miss Piddlewinks, taught her as a youngster, called the gift of the acorn.

"If you aren't greedy," her grandmother had said, "and if you plant more than you will eat during the season, there will always be trees and food for generations to come, for squirrels, birds and all kinds of creatures. So don't be selfish," her grandmother had told her, tapping Ozette's nose with the tip of her sharp claw.

Ozette thought about her grandmother and her life before coming to Farlandia. For generations, Ozette's relatives had lived in a distant part of Earth World. From stories her grandmother related, the forests had originally been much like the ones in Farlandia, filled with animals, old-growth trees, clear rivers and streams and rich in beauty and abundant food.

Unfortunately, that had all changed shortly after Ozette was born. Terrifying noises had echoed through the forests and those brave enough to investigate had discovered large, yellow metal monsters like nothing they'd ever seen before. The monsters roared through the woods, uprooting ancient trees and scraping fields of vibrantly colored wildflowers bare until there was nothing but dirt that turned to mud when it rained.

Gone were the blackberry brambles and fruit-bearing trees where generations of squirrels and birds had feasted. Pristine streams now ran brown with silt. Soon the once-beautiful land was almost barren. Trees and fields of flowers were replaced with large houses. The pathways the animals had used were covered with black, shiny material where nothing grew.

Large creatures, which her grandmother had called humans, took over more and more of the land. They began wandering into what remained of the forest, carrying long, black sticks that belched smoke. Pheasants, quail, deer and squirrels fell victim to these loud, smoking sticks. The animals retreated farther and farther into the forest. But the humans were never far behind.

When Ozette was old enough to understand, her grandmother explained what had happened. As a result of the humans, the food supply was severely reduced and areas safe to seek food were growing smaller and smaller. This was why the gift of the acorn was so important. Soon, squirrels were burying all kinds of nuts, hoping to replenish the supply. Birds were working diligently to spread and scatter flower seeds, hoping for fresh crops. The idyllic life in the forest was slowly turning into a fight for survival. Many were leaving, not sure where they were going, but knowing they couldn't remain.

How Ozette missed her grandmother! She'd had the reputation of being very wise, in part because she could see into the future. Sometimes when they were planting, her grandmother's ears would perk up and she would carefully sniff an acorn or other nut. Then, instead of planting it, she would bite into it, examine it carefully and make her proclamation.

"Ahh. Looks like your Auntie Bets will be having triplets, come early fall. All girls," she once said, smiling broadly. And it came to pass. She could predict frigid winters, food shortages, sweltering summers and even helpful and trivial events. Ozette sighed. There was another memory playing in the back of her mind, but she couldn't quite catch it as it flitted through her squirrelly brain.

Because of her grandmother, Ozette had vowed to be the best tree-planting squirrel around. She would pick up a nut in her paws and roll it around, sniffing it to make sure it was tasty. Using her front feet, with their sharp toenails, she would drill it into the ground. From behind she looked like a miniature jack-hammer. Then she would smooth the dirt, cover the spot with leaves and move on. Of course, she always took time to eat a few of the tasty morsels. She did need to keep up her strength, after all!

Chapter Six

THE WORD IS OUT

Maxwell may have been handsome and powerful, but he was a terrible gossip. While Ozette was busy planting trees, news of her adventure was spreading rapidly through Farlandia. Everyone was excitedly discussing this turn of events.

Tired from her planting, Ozette returned to her tree hoping for a quick nap. To her delight, Sydney, one of her fairy friends, had left a hand-woven vine basket filled with freshly picked carrots at the tree's base. She was munching away happily when she heard the sound of wings.

She looked up and saw a large group of fairies and elves flitting her way.

Then she heard a chattering commotion in the trees and saw her squirrel friends, leaping through the branches.

They were joined by birds, a white unicorn and dozens of other woodland creatures making their way to her tall maple tree.

"Queen Ozette! Queen Ozette! Queen Ozette!" they chanted loudly.

Ozette shook her paw at them, saying, "That Maxwell is such a blabbermouth. There is no Queen Ozette. Just me, plain Ozette," she chided them.

Oliver came forward, obviously the self-proclaimed spokes-elf. "Queen Beatrix has deeded the land to itself and made you the caretaker. You've been gifted a tiara, a crown. In our book, that makes you a queen!" he parroted Maxwell.

Ozette put her paws on her hips. "A squirrel can't be a queen, Oliver," she said. "Only humans are royalty."

"Au contraire, my squirrelly friend," Oliver countered. "Duchess Zorina is a dog and she's royalty. A queen is a leader, someone who loves the land and all who dwell on it. That would be you, Ozette."

"We would be honored to have a squirrel as our queen," said Maggie, a sweet-natured unicorn.

"Being a white squirrel makes you special, and our queen should be special," added red squirrel twins, Zoe and Chloe, in unison. The other animals nodded in agreement and a raccoon gave Ozette a thumbs up sign.

Muttering about that "gossiping Maxwell" under her breath, Ozette doled out the treats sent by the cook to all her friends. Then she waved the animals away, saying she would "think about it." Her nap forgotten, she started planting more nuts.

Ozette was almost finished when the princess's golden retriever, Cassady, bounded up to her carrying a basket in her mouth. Behind her was Princess Abrianna, clothed in a long, purple dress with white and yellow daisies pinned in her flowing silver hair.

Ozette didn't know many humans, but she liked Princess Abrianna because she was kind and didn't act superior to non-humans. And, she often brought Ozette special treats.

Princess Abrianna took the basket from Cassady's mouth and handed it to Ozette.

Ozette pulled away the dainty yellow

napkin cover to reveal freshly baked pecan-wal-nut-almond-veggie smackaroons, one of Ozette's favorite treats.

"Mmmm," she said offering some also to Cassady and Abrianna.

The three friends munched in silence. Suddenly Princess Abrianna spoke.

"I hear you've had quite an adventure."

Ozette nodded, not wanting to talk with her mouth full.

"Queen Beatrix adores that dog like a child, Ozette. You should be honored she has made you caretaker of Farlandia. Ozette, have you any idea what can happen to land and its creatures? Even here, in beautiful Farlandia, our cousin wanted to build a hunting lodge and clear forests for crops. Do you realize what that means? To the old-growth trees that would be cut? To the pristine creeks and rivers that could be polluted? To the animals that would lose their homes and even their lives?"

Ozette nodded her head anxiously. She was painfully aware of what could happen to the land, but she let the princess have her say.

Princess Abrianna knelt down and took Ozette's paw. "There are humans who see nature as something to be exploited. They are greedy and never satisfied. They don't care about the animals, elves, fairies, plants, streams and trees. It's a great honor that has been bestowed upon you, as caretaker of Farlandia, and a big responsibility.

"As queen, you'll have a certain authority. You'll be a fine ruler, Ozette, and I am very happy for you and all of us. You care intensely for the land and all who dwell there. This, Ozette, is your destiny," she said, looking deeply into Ozette's eyes.

And with that, she called Cassady and headed home.

Ozette climbed her nesting tree, stretched out on a branch, scratched her left ear and thought about what the princess had said.

"Destiny," she whispered. Why did that sound familiar? Ozette tried not to think about her past, but suddenly the memory that had been evading her came to her in a flash.

She and The Divine Miss Piddlewinks had been busily planting acorns as the trees wept scarlet and gold leaves and succulent acorns. Suddenly her grandmother had gasped. Ozette hurried over to her and found her rolling a shiny golden acorn in her paws. Ozette had never seen anything like it before.

Her grandmother nodded thoughtfully and

said, "I've long suspected this, Ozette. A white squirrel is rarely born into our family. Have you ever wondered why the rest of your family is gray?"

Ozette shook her head. She had just accepted that she was what she was, a white squirrel.

"This golden acorn is the sign I've been hoping for. Acorns hold many secrets. But this acorn, Ozette, holds one of the most amazing secrets of all. Look at me, child," she ordered as she placed the golden acorn into Ozette's paw.

The gold sparkled in the sunlight, and Ozette could feel her paw becoming warm and tingly beneath the acorn.

Ozette looked into her grandmother's wise eyes and felt mesmerized, even a little dizzy.

"Ah, yes. You have a destiny, a wonderful destiny," her grandmother said. "When the time is right, you'll remember this day."

The Divine Miss Piddlewinks paused, her paw covering the one in which Ozette held the golden acorn. She stared straight ahead, deep in thought, and then turned back to Ozette.

"Your destiny is not here, my child. Our forest is disappearing and can no longer provide you the home you deserve. Your destiny is far away, in a lovely forest much like ours used to be."

"But – "

"There is no question. You cannot realize your destiny here. You must leave soon. The hunters continue to come, and they will be seeking those with the white fur."

Ozette stubbornly shook her head and stuck out her furry chin.

The Divine Miss Piddlewinks closed Ozette's tingling paw tight around the golden acorn and stroked Ozette's soft white head.

"Ozette, the stress of being around so many humans and having their homes destroyed has made many of the animals angry," her grandmother said. "They are looking for a scapegoat to blame. More and more of the animals are saying life was fine until a white squirrel was born. They are blaming the destruction on you, saying you are bad luck."

Ozette's mouth dropped open in shock.

"Nothing could be farther from the truth, Ozette. You must believe me," her grandmother said.

Ozette nodded, looking sad.

"We will begin preparations this evening. You will carry the golden acorn with you, and it will guide you to the far away land where your destiny awaits."

"How can I leave you?" Ozette asked, tears filling her eyes.

"Ah, my beloved," her grandmother smiled. "When you feel the wind ruffling your fur, I will be there. When you gaze at a starry sky, I will be there. When you catch the scent of wildflowers or see a sunrise that takes your breath away, I will be there. We will meet again. I promise."

Despite Ozette's sadness at having to leave her family and the few friends who remained in the forest, she obeyed her grandmother. The acorn had, in fact, guided her to Farland and then farther on to the deep woods of Farlandia. When she had reached the forest there, the golden acorn had stopped tingling in her paw, and she knew she had found her new home. Remembering her grandmother's story of the gift of the acorn, she'd planted the golden nut nearby, not far from the tall maple tree where she now lived.

Why had she just now remembered this? Her grandmother had declared she had a wonderful destiny. The golden acorn had led her here and was planted nearby. Although she was the only white squirrel in the forest, she'd been accepted by her new friends. She had learned to love and care for all other creatures, and even the one human in their midst.

Her destiny. Was it to become named Queen of Farlandia and protect this magical place? She scurried to the spot where she had planted the golden acorn, saw the tiniest sprout pushing its way through the once-bare ground. She smiled and returned to her tree.

Above her, birds twittered and fluttered to and fro. From her vantage point, she also could see countless small creatures below, scurrying through the forest. Each so unique, so vulnerable. She did love this land and all its inhabitants. If she did decide to be Queen Ozette, she vowed to protect them with her life. But she wouldn't build a castle. Her cozy nest would do just fine.

She had to admit the tiara was splendid. She dug it out of her nest and tried it on. She darted down the tree to the nearby pond, which was as smooth as a looking glass and ringed with spring flowers. She peered into the water.

"Oh my," she whispered. She truly did look like a queen in the tiara. The gold and jewels sparkled and looked lovely, against her shining white fur.

"But it would be pretentious to wear it, wouldn't it?" she whispered guiltily.

She rushed up her tree and hid it behind her stash of dried fruits, unaware that Oliver, Ariel and

Sydney had seen her at the pond and were happily making plans for her coronation.

The next morning, Ozette's friends again gathered under her nesting tree, just as the sun was peeking over the horizon.

Ozette heard them whispering at the base of her tree. She stretched, gave her tail a quick grooming and rushed down to meet them. They looked at her expectantly.

"OK. I'll do it. I'll be queen, but I don't want my life to change in any way. No castles. No servants. No bowing and curtsying," she said sternly, pushing aside doubts that she had what it took to be a queen.

Her friends jumped up and down with happiness.

"We always have a party in the spring to celebrate the return of new life in the forest," Oliver said, smiling broadly and rubbing his hands together in anticipation. "That will be the perfect time for your coronation."

"Oliver, don't you dare make a big deal out of this," Ozette said, shaking a paw at him. "However, a small, simple gathering might be nice," she said.

Soon, all of Farlandia was atwitter with plans for the annual Spring Fling. Ozette refused to call it a coronation and begged her friends to downplay that aspect of it. They all solemnly promised, but if Ozette had been paying more attention, she would have noticed each time they agreed, they would also hold their hands, claws or paws behind their backs with fingers crossed.

Ozette insisted she be allowed to help with the planning of the Spring Fling, which would take place in three weeks on the full moon.

Discussions of decorations, food, dancing and games continued far into the night, with all the elves, fairies and animals having a say. Sometimes, Ozette's walnut-sized brain didn't think it could hold one more idea.

Chapter Seven

UP THE CREEK WITH A PADDLE

In typical squirrel fashion, it was hard for Ozette to focus on one thing for too long. On this sun-drenched spring morning, she was stretched out on a fat branch of her massive maple tree picking bits of pecans from her teeth by chewing on a twig, like her grandmother had taught her, using the fibers as squirrelly dental floss. A light breeze ruffled her soft fur, and she felt her grandmother's presence as she so often did when she quieted her mind.

Ozette loved spring, and had chosen this tree because she could lie in her nesting hole or on a branch and gaze at nature's patchwork quilt of colors. She hadn't realized there were so many shades of green!

She loved making up names for the many wildflowers that grew in the forest. Today she spied Tinkerbells, Fairy Wings, Sunsprites, Magenta Happies and Pinkettes. At least that's what she called them.

She yawned, stood up and started waving her tail back and forth, flagging messages to the other squirrels in Farlandia.

"CRRK! CRRK!" she called.

She heard an answering call from a nearby oak tree and recognized her squirrel friend Daphne's "THROAK! THROAK."

Ozette dashed down the tree, stopping only to snag a mouthful of violets that grew in the shade of her maple.

The two squirrels met under an apple tree, where Daphne was crunching on a patch of chickweed and spring mushrooms. Ozette joined her, munching in a comfortable silence until they were both full.

"Let's do something fun," Ozette said. "It's too nice a day to waste lounging around and I'm weary of planning the Spring Fling."

The two squirrels decided to make a bark raft and float down the creek. The trees were so thick they could scamper from limb to limb, all the way to the water, without touching the ground. They paused only for a tender leaf or bud snack, when the mood struck.

They soon reached the creek, and Ozette shook her head. Recent rains had swelled the usually placid creek, and Ozette thought it was too swift to paddle.

"Don't be such a spoilsport," Daphne taunted. "It will be great fun!"

Ozette reluctantly relented, and the two found a sturdy piece of oak bark big enough to hold them. They searched for short branches they could fashion into paddles.

They were ready to launch their little raft, when Oliver came scrambling through the woods wearing a red backpack, his wings tucked behind the straps. "Let me go, too!" he begged.

"I don't think it's big enough for all of us, Oliver," Ozette said.

Oliver hung his head and twitched his pointed elf ears. "We can fit! I know we can! Please, Ozette," he begged.

"Let him come," Daphne said. "We could use

another paddler in this current."

Against her better judgment, Ozette helped Oliver make a paddle, and soon they had launched the raft into the fast-moving water.

"Whee!" shouted Daphne, as the makeshift raft careened through the water.

Trees and sky rushed by, and Ozette found herself having fun, despite her misgivings. They startled a deer drinking at the creek's edge as they drifted by, and a flock of sparrows took flight when they saw the raft. A low-flying griffin tipped its wings to them as it caught an updraft and glided over the creek.

After paddling until the sun was high in the sky, they decided to stop for a snack. They beached the bark raft and stretched. It had been a little cramped for the three of them on the small craft.

"I've some goodies in my backpack," Oliver said, slipping the bright red pack from his back.

Ozette grinned. Oliver was famous for never leaving home without a stash of freshly baked treats.

The trio sat on the bank, and Oliver unpacked a bag of sun-dried strawberries, chocolate neener neeners and cherry fruitinas.

"Yum yum!" Daphne exclaimed, stuffing a

chocolate neener neener in her mouth, crumbs raining down her furry chin.

"It's a good thing squirrels are as active as they are. You can sure tuck into some food," Oliver said.

Ozette looked at him primly. "We've very high metabolisms, and I never gain an ounce," she said.

Daphne nodded her head in agreement, as she reached for a sun-dried strawberry.

They drank from the stream and piled back onto the raft.

"This section might be a tad tricky," Daphne said. "Do exactly as I say."

They came to an area of swift-running rapids, with large rocks peeking out of the creek.

"Maybe we should carry the raft around these rapids instead of risking getting dumped," Ozette said, nervously eying the churning white water.

But Daphne remained focused on paddling between two huge rocks.

"Paddle left, Oliver! Hard!" Daphne shouted, as they came to a rapid.

Confused, Oliver paddled to the right.

"Left! Not right!" Ozette yelled at the panicking elf.

They hit a large rock broadside, spun around

three times and were catapulted into the icy creek. Squirrels are naturally good swimmers, and they headed for shore.

"Help!"

Ozette turned and saw Oliver flailing in the creek. "Swim toward me, Oliver!" she shouted.

"I can't swim!" he yelled, as his head disappeared under water.

"I thought all elves were required to take swimming lessons!" Daphne yelled, as she watched Oliver surface.

"He must have skipped that day, Daphne," Ozette said dryly, turning to swim back to Oliver.

The elf grabbed Ozette, threatening to pull them both under.

"Stop fighting me, Oliver," Ozette said. "Grab my tail and I'll tow you to shore."

But the frightened elf kept struggling, and Ozette feared they would both drown. "Give me a paw here, Daphne!" Ozette shouted for back-up.

Daphne headed to the struggling pair, but she, too, was growing tired from fighting the current. Both Ozette and Oliver slipped from the surface.

Daphne heard a "thwomp ... thwomp" and looked up to see a bald eagle, heading for the seemingly doomed pair. The eagle was late heading home to relieve his spouse. It was his turn to watch their chicks while she fed, and he knew he was already in for a tongue lashing. But he had scruples and wasn't about to ignore the plight of the animals in the water. Besides, he recognized Ozette. The eagle was hoping to snag an invitation to the coronation party and knew it would be bad form not to help the guest of honor.

He swooped low over the water, as Oliver and Ozette surfaced again. "Grab my wings and hold on!" he ordered. Ozette and Oliver each grabbed a wing and soon were airborne.

The eagle carried them to shore on his strong wings and set them down in a grassy clearing. Daphne came running, tripping over tree roots, to reach her friends. The eagle shrugged away their words of gratitude and headed skyward, muttering, "Crazy kids to think they could raft in that raging creek."

The sun was beginning to set, and the three drenched friends headed toward home. Oliver was shivering and had lost his backpack in the swollen creek. No matter, since the remaining goodies would have been soaked.

Ozette and Daphne helped the elf climb through and over the tree branches until they reached his little stone cottage nestled under a towering hickory tree. Like all elf and fairy houses, Oliver's home was a whimsical hodgepodge of turrets, cupolas, bay windows and porches. Window boxes were filled to overflowing with moss and a profusion of colorful flowers. On the door hung a wreath of bird feathers, gifted to Oliver by his many winged friends. Ozette was always charmed by his home.

"Come in, and I'll fix some tea and dinner for us," Oliver said, opening the door. Soaked, hungry and cold, the two squirrels took him up on his offer.

Oliver gathered kindling and logs and started a fire in his river-stone fireplace. The friends dried and warmed themselves at the hearth. Oliver might not be a good swimmer, but he was a great cook and soon had set plates of spinach quichette and roasted vegetable razzle-dazzles in front of them as a pot of strong elderberry tea brewed over the fire. Soon the friends were dry, warm and satisfied.

Ozette dozed in front of the fire until Daphne poked her with a paw.

"Time to head back to our nests," Daphne sighed, getting up. They hugged Oliver good night and headed out into the crisp, clear night to their homes.

Chapter Eight

SKYDIVING, MINUS THE PARACHUTE

Early the next morning, Ozette started down her tree, periodically stretching, yawning and pausing to enjoy the streaks of pink, gold and crimson splashed across the sky.

Suddenly she heard "gallump, gallump, gallump" and looked up to see Cassady bounding through the woods, ears flapping, tongue lolling out of her mouth. The large golden dog stopped, gave Ozette a wet lick and then proceeded to root around in the vine basket to see if any carrots remained from the gift Sydney had left days before.

Princess Abrianna was charging through the woods, calling for her dog. Her hair was flowing down her back, blowing in the breeze as she ran. She giggled as she grabbed Cassady by the scruff of her neck and wiped Ozette's wet face with the hem of her silky crimson skirt.

"Sorry about that, Ozette," she apologized. "She got away from me. But I'll make it up to you. The bees have offered me honey from their hives. We'll bake honeyhunkettes for the Spring Fling," she said with a wink.

Ozette smiled. Honeyhunkettes would be perfect! She watched her friend walk briskly down the path and thought how lucky she was to live in such a delightful forest.

Ozette spent the morning cleaning her nest. Queen or not, she sure did get messy. Soon bits of walnut shells, old acorns, fruit and vegetable tidbits and scraps of withered leaves were raining onto the ground from above. As a bonus, she found some still edible dried apples, a piece of yellow cloth and two cardinal feathers she had forgotten she'd stashed in the back of her nest.

She scrambled through the treetops, using her sharp teeth to cut a leaf here, a leaf there, for her nest. What a wonderful variety of leaves the forest provided! She tucked them neatly into her home, and then ambled down her tree to collect fresh moss for carpeting, taking only small amounts from each patch so the plants weren't harmed. She made numerous trips back and forth, carrying the moss in her mouth. After she had smoothed the moss neatly on the floor of her nest, she admired her tidy home. Feeling pleased, she tucked herself under her pile of fresh leaves and fell into a deep sleep.

She was dreaming about riding Maxwell through the forest when she heard whispers at the bottom of her tree.

"She's been so busy with the Spring Fling plans, she'll be mad if we wake her."

"Not Ozette. She'll be mad if she misses out," said another familiar voice.

Ozette's ears pricked up, and she stuck her head out of her nest. Five of her squirrel friends were gathered at the base of the tree – Daphne, Chloe and Zoe, Guido and Baby Fiona, who was still a tiny youngster.

"We're going adventuring and want you to join us," called Baby Fiona.

Adventuring was a term the squirrels used when they took to the treetops, never touching the ground. These aerial highways were beloved by all tree-dwelling creatures, but especially the squirrels.

Ozette clapped her paws. "Sounds wonderful. Shall we pack a picnic?" she asked.

"There should be plenty of food along the way, but we might want to pack a few snacks," Guido answered.

"But what can we carry it in?" asked the ever-practical Chloe.

"Hmm." Ozette thought a minute and grabbed the piece of bright yellow cloth she had found when cleaning her nest. "We can put food in the cloth, fold it up and attach it to one of us. Sort of a squirrelly backpack," Ozette said, remembering the backpack Oliver had lost in the creek.

"I want to wear it. I've never had a backpack," squealed Baby Fiona.

Ozette fashioned the cloth into a makeshift backpack, filled it with nuts and seeds and tied it around Baby Fiona's chest. Off they scrambled through the trees, stopping to munch on buds and early fruits and having a wonderful outing.

Ariel joined them, chattering non-stop about the coronation, as she darted from tree to tree with them. Below, they could see other fairies, flitting on their iridescent wings. They waved to the squirrels and wished them well.

Suddenly, disaster struck.

The ties on Baby Fiona's backpack caught on the end of a branch. The harder she tugged, the tighter the knot became. She started to cry.

Ozette put on her thinking cap and soon came up with a plan. She plucked one of last fall's remaining hickory nuts from the tree and started sharpening her teeth, paying special attention to her incisors.

"I'll cut the ties with my trusty teeth," she said. "Guido, you're the strongest. Get on the branch below and catch Baby Fiona."

Ozette easily gnawed through the strings. Unfortunately, she had never taken physics and knew nothing about wind speed or trajectory.

As the ties came loose, the hapless young squirrel tumbled past Guido and down to the pond below, nuts and seeds raining down alongside her. Fortunately, Baby Fiona was still clutching the fabric, which billowed like a parachute, slowing her down long enough for Ozette to sound a piercing "HELP!" to anyone below.

As Baby Fiona almost reached the water, Mateo, one of the fastest and most athletic elves in the woodlands, had been sunning himself on the grassy banks of the pond. He rocketed down the banks as fast as his elfin legs could carry him and dove cleanly into the water. Baby Fiona landed in the pond with a splash and disappeared beneath the surface, her bright yellow parachute floating listlessly on top. Silence fell over the pond.

It seemed like an eternity passed until Mateo finally burst through the surface holding a sputtering, bedraggled, very thankful baby squirrel.

One of the eldest and most nurturing fairies in the forest, Sydney, had been fluttering nearby, gathering honeysuckle for tea. She rushed to dry the shivering pair with her filmy wings. While all the friends hugged Baby Fiona and congratulated brave Mateo, Ozette stood alone to the side, her head hanging dejectedly as she replayed the last few minutes in her mind and realized how close they had come to a tragedy. She slowly turned to leave and started down the path toward home alone.

Also on the same path, but coming from the opposite direction, Oliver was out for a stroll, having just completed his first swimming lesson. He was quite pleased with himself. His teacher had told him that he did very well and, at his next lesson, he might even be ready to stick his *other* foot into the water too. As he rounded the bend, he almost ran straight into Ozette.

"Ozette! Why are you crying?" Oliver asked, taking his friend's paw in his elfin hands.

Between sobs, Ozette explained the disaster with Baby Fiona.

"I don't deserve to be queen," she said, pushing the thought of the small sprout and her grandmother's words from her mind. "I want to cancel the Spring Fling and forget this whole crazy idea."

"Sweet Ozette," Oliver said, patting her shoulder. "It wasn't your fault. It was an accident. Squirrels are great acrobats in the trees, but sometimes they take a tumble. But they get right back up and start all over again."

Ozette shook her head silently, her fuzzy chin trembling and her dark eyes pooling up with tears.

Just then, they heard a chattering in the trees. They looked up and saw Baby Fiona, Guido, Daphne, Zoe and Chloe scrambling down a cherry tree. Baby Fiona was in the lead, chattering in a high squeaky voice and bursting with excitement.

"Ozette! That was the most fun I've had since that wind storm when my nest flew from tree to tree with me still in it!"

"Fun?! Fun?! I was so afraid that my carelessness had scared, or even worse, hurt you," Ozette said, her eyes widening in surprise.

Baby Fiona hugged Ozette. "This was so exciting that I want to do it again. All I need is some fashion, um, I mean *safety,* accessories like a little helmet and parachute. Skydiving, here I come!"

Ozette wasn't sure she could envision a squirrel sailing through the skies with a parachute, but sometimes she knew enough to keep her opinions to herself.

Chapter Nine

SKYDIVING SQUIRRELS

Several days passed, and heavy rains kept Ozette from completing her usual outdoor tasks. But she didn't mind since she knew the rain nourished the thirsty earth. She smiled when she thought of her little golden acorn sprout drinking in the fat raindrops to help it grow. When she did venture forth in the wet weather, she curled her fluffy tail over her head like an umbrella and took pleasure in letting raindrops splash on her bright pink tongue.

But, as it always did, sunshine eventually

returned and green growth abounded through the forest.

Ozette was enjoying the warm sunshine and had just finished harvesting some early greens and mushrooms from the forest when a shiny iridescent blur came hurtling through the sky and landed at her feet. Stunned, Ozette stared down at the small mound of silver gauzy material, when suddenly out popped Baby Fiona's grinning face.

"Like it?" she asked, jumping up and turning in circles.

"Amazing," Ozette said smiling, "Wherever did you get such a beautiful contraption?"

"I talked some spiders into spinning the fabric," said Baby Fiona proudly. "Had to collect lots of bugs for them in exchange though," she shuddered. "And then Sydney sewed it into a parachute with wings, kind of like the fairies have, only custom made for me. All that's left on my list is a helmet. Any ideas?"

Ozette tapped her paw to her lips and thought. And thought. And thought.

Suddenly, she held up a paw. "Perhaps we could fasten some empty walnut shells together with something sticky. That might work."

She climbed to her nest and rummaged through her stash of nuts. She found two large walnuts, threw them down to Baby Fiona and raced back down the tree. She and Baby Fiona carefully cracked the nuts, making sure to keep each half intact.

"There's some sticky sap on that tree over there," Ozette said, pointing to a pine. "Let's stick the shells together with that and shape it to fit your head."

The squirrels worked carefully, until they had fashioned a helmet of walnut shells.

Baby Fiona beamed and took off her parachute. "Thanks, Ozette. I want you to be the first to try it, since you inspired me to achieve this dream. If it weren't for you, I never would have had this opportunity," Baby Fiona said.

Ozette grimaced. She wasn't sure about this skydiving.

When she saw Ozette hesitate, a mischievous twinkle came into Baby Fiona's eyes. "I would think a queen would want to be adventurous," she said, playing on Ozette's pride. "Think of the stories you can tell at your coronation."

Ozette knew she would never live it down if she didn't try, so she put on the parachute and the walnut helmet and started to climb up a small tree.

"No! That tree over there," Baby Fiona said, pointing to a tall red oak.

With some misgivings, Ozette reluctantly climbed up the tree. When she reached the top, she looked down. Being a squirrel, she wasn't afraid of heights, but she was going to have to let go of the top limb and trust that the parachute would open. Her honor was at stake. If young Baby Fiona could do it, so could she.

She made sure the helmet and parachute were fastened properly, took a deep breath, thrust out her chin and jumped. As she slowly drifted downward, she noticed the silence. Still and calm, it was a friendly silence, as though the forest was watching her fly.

She drifted lazily past a black crow that cawed, "Welcome to the club. Now you know how it feels!"

A surprised sloth stopped his munching and slowly gazed upward.

She drifted past a dozing raccoon couple, a dragon meticulously grooming herself and a nest of baby birds who watched her with beaks agape.

Suddenly, she felt something solid. She had landed on the top of a sapling, her parachute folding around her like a cloak.

"That was such fun! Now I know why you wanted to skydive!" she chattered excitedly as Baby Fiona ran up the tree.

"You looked majestic," said Baby Fiona. "Want to try it again?"

Checking the position of the sun, Ozette shook her head. "Another time. Oliver has invited me for lunch and has promised pecan yummettes for dessert." She took off the helmet and parachute and handed them to Baby Fiona. The young squirrel donned them in a flash and scrambled to the top of a tall hickory.

Ozette watched Baby Fiona's parachute catch the wind and slowly float down. She smiled as she thought of the good that had eventually come from such a scary day. "Hmm," she grinned. "I just might take up skydiving too someday."

Chapter Ten

THE METAMORPHOSIS OF OLIVER

When she reached Oliver's cottage, he was setting the table with his finest china. Ozette's pink nose wiggled as she sniffed the delectable scents. "Something smells awfully good," she said.

Oliver smiled his broadest smile. "Pecan-stuffed mushrooms, first-greens-of-spring salad, lemonette linguine, pecan yummettes and mint tea," he proclaimed proudly.

Ozette licked her lips in anticipation.

The two friends chatted happily as they ate the beautifully prepared lunch. Ozette told Oliver about her skydiving experience and how magical she felt. Oliver smiled slyly, hoping her sense of adventure would prevail when he offered her a truly magical experience.

"After lunch, I want to show you something," he said, taking her paw and squeezing it. They finished their meal in a companionable silence. Then Oliver left the room and returned with three vials of pale green liquid in his hands. The small, square vials were fashioned from crystal with oval-shaped stoppers carved from oak. Ozette looked at him, puzzled.

"Ozette, you know that I'm the fourth cousin, twice removed, from Shape-Shifter Elf," he said solemnly.

Ozette nodded, vaguely remembering Oliver telling her that he came from a family with special talents. Although she had never met Shape-Shifter Elf, he was said to be quite eccentric and loved to dabble in white magic.

"He's been teaching me to do magical things."

Ozette frowned. She knew that Oliver could be impulsive and wondered where this conversation was leading.

"It's quite wonderful. There are formulas for

making potions that let you change your shape and become something else."

Seeing Ozette's look of alarm, he hastily said, "It's only for four hours. Then you return to your original self."

"Oliver, you shouldn't be tampering with such things. What if you get stuck as something else and can't get back?"

"That won't happen," he said confidently, puffing out his chest. "I followed the formulas perfectly."

Ozette shook her head skeptically as Oliver showed her the vials.

She squinted and read the labels: "Hummingbird Potion, Butterfly Potion, Cardinal Potion...well, I suppose there are *worse* things you could turn into," she said grudgingly.

"Want to try one, Ozette?"

She shook her head vehemently. "Not me, Oliver. Oh no. Not me. I'm perfectly content to be who I am. I like me."

"Ah, come on," he cajoled. "Don't you ever long to be something other than what you are? We can both try it together."

Ozette thought of a brilliant response to end the discussion. "I'm going to be crowned queen at the Spring Fling soon. I can't risk it," she said, trying to sound haughty so that Oliver would stop trying to coax her.

"But I thank you kindly for the most delicious lunch," she said, hugging her friend and hoping she hadn't hurt his feelings. She paused at the door. "Oliver," she said, holding his hand in her paws, "I care about you. I don't want anything to happen to you. Please forget these potions."

Oliver averted his eyes as he hugged her back.

As she headed into the forest, Ozette didn't hear him whisper, "You'll see, Ozette. I'll show you that it can be fun."

The rest of the day passed quietly, and Ozette was up early the next morning. She was lounging on a limb, enjoying the warmth of the sun on her back and counting how many species of flowers she could see without turning her head.

Deep in thought, she was busily making up names for the newly blooming wildflowers.

"Yellow Deedledots…Blue Starbrights… Fairybreaths," she recited.

She was feeling most content when a brilliant blue butterfly landed on her right ear. Then it was dancing on her nose, making it itch. When she tried to shoo it away with her paw, she heard laughter. Familiar laughter. She shook her head, trying to dislodge the butterfly. More laughter. Puzzled, she looked closer at the creature.

"Don't you recognize me?" it giggled.

"What? Who are you? Your voice sounds familiar."

The butterfly hovered over her head. "It's me. Oliver!"

Ozette clapped a paw to her mouth in disbelief!

Oliver did a few dips and swirls, then landed again on Ozette's nose. "This is such fun, Ozette! Do you have any idea how delicious it is to sip nectar? And flitting here and there is such fun. These wings are much stronger than my elf ones! Don't you think I am so handsome?" He was so excited he hardly took a breath between all his words.

Ozette nodded cautiously. "Uh huh. So, when will you be an elf again?" she asked.

"I took it around sunrise, so it should be wearing off soon," he said. "See you later. Wheeeee!" And off he fluttered.

If Ozette were honest, she would have admitted that she was just a little envious. She thought back to her skydiving experience, and what a thrill it had been.

But she forced her thoughts away from such

silliness. No potions for her! The Spring Fling was coming up, and she couldn't risk doing something foolish. She was going to be a queen, after all.

She slept fitfully that night. Oliver's question, "Don't you ever long to be something other than what you are?" kept lingering in her mind.

She loved being a squirrel. She loved scampering through the treetops and having a fluffy tail to groom, even though Oliver teased her that it looked like a bottle brush.

Still, Oliver was having such fun. All night, the thought flitted around in her mind like a tempting little blue butterfly.

Chapter Eleven

A DELICIOUS OPPORTUNITY?

Ozette was up at first light. After carefully grooming herself, she headed to Oliver's cottage to make sure her friend was all right.

"Ozette," he said, opening the door and yawning. He was clad in sky blue boxer shorts embroidered with fire-breathing dragons, and his short, dark curly hair was in disarray over his elfin ears. He obviously had not been awake long.

"Have some breakfast with an elf-turned-butterfly-turned-elf-again," he said, laughing.

Ozette smiled sheepishly. All of her worries had been for nothing.

While they enjoyed a light breakfast, Oliver regaled her with his experiences as a butterfly, including the delicious nectar he had sipped and the beautiful flowers he had visited.

"Come on, Ozette! You've never seen anything like an up-close look at these flowery gems. So intricate and colorful! You would love it! It will be an enchanting experience for you!" He could tell Ozette was weakening.

"Well...I suppose...if it's just for a few hours...it might be sort of fun," she mused. "But I would still be afraid that I wouldn't turn back into a squirrel." She poured a second cup of lemon balm tea and daintily munched an acorn croquette.

"But look at me!" he twirled around. "I'm back and the better for it. Now which would you like to try first – hummingbird or cardinal?"

Ozette started to shake her head but a distant memory flitted into her squirrelly mind. She was a mere babe, just getting her first fur, and her eyes were still closed. Her grandmother, The Divine Miss Piddlewinks, was holding her on her knee.

"Ozette, never forget this," she said with a gleam in her eye. "There are old squirrels and there are bold squirrels. But there are no old, bold squirrels. Sometimes, my precious one, you must choose. Being prudent is usually wise, but never let fear keep you from experiencing the delicious opportunities life will offer you."

She then kissed Ozette with a brief lick on the nose, a special sign of affection she gave only to her granddaughter.

Ozette gulped as her vision cleared and she saw Oliver looking at her expectantly. Was this one of those delicious opportunities?

"Hmm," she said, picking up the vials from the table. Cardinals were certainly striking with their brilliant red plumage, but Ozette loved the way hummingbirds flitted from flower to flower, and their shimmering feathers glistened in the sun. "If I were to do this," she said, "I would want to be a hummingbird."

"Great choice, Ozette," Oliver said. "If you take this now, I can watch you change."

"Oliver, I still don't know if I want to do this. I love being a squirrel!"

"It's only for a short time, Ozette. Think of the stories you can tell your friends."

Like all squirrels, Ozette was sometimes prone to rash decisions.

"OK!" she said excitedly. "But please check on

me later to make sure I return to being a squirrel again. Promise?"

Oliver clapped his hand over his heart. "Promise!"

Ozette uncapped the vial and looked at the pale green potion. She sniffed it. It smelled like strawberries. She took a deep breath and drank the liquid.

"Let's head outside," Oliver said as he led Ozette into the garden.

She was already feeling a little strange.

"Oliver," she said, her voice more of a soft squeak than her usual chitter. "I feel weird. And I don't think it's a good weird, either."

Ozette started changing before Oliver's eyes. Her white fur slowly dissolved and became glimmering green feathers, with touches of vivid scarlet at her throat. Tiny wings sprouted on her back, and a long, thin beak replaced her mouth and nose. She stood there on the ground, flapping her little wings.

"That's it, Ozette! You're a hummingbird! See those flowers over there?" he asked, pointing toward a sea of red. "Try those."

Ozette flapped her wings vigorously. She rose ever so slowly at first, then flew faster and faster as she gained confidence. Her wings were flapping eighty times a second. She flew in great circles, dipping, flitting, diving and even flying upside down, which made her a little dizzy.

She waved a wing at Oliver and headed deeper into the garden, where she hovered over a brilliant scarlet flower and, using her minuscule grooved tongue, lapped the sweet nectar from the bloom. Oliver had been right about the delicious nectar. Each kind of flower had such a unique taste.

"Yum!" Ozette's taste buds felt like they were exploding as she sampled the nectar from a different deep pink trumpet-shaped flower. "Sort of a raspberry burst with violet undertones."

She flitted through the woods, stopping every few minutes to sip more nectar. She thought squirrels ate often, but she had never been this hungry before. She wondered how these birds ever had time to do important things like planting acorns, going rafting or adventuring. Then she remembered that she had never seen hummingbirds do any of these things and she was grateful to really be a squirrel.

As she flew over the pond, she saw a group of elves in swimsuits gathering for a late morning swim. She recognized Oliver, Mateo and Barnaby as, one by one, they dove into the pond. She tried to get Oliver's attention by hovering overhead, but he didn't notice her and dove into the pond, splashing cold water high into the air. With his lithe body, he had proven to be a natural swimmer, and Ozette was happy to see what great progress he had made.

She shook off the cold splash and flew over to a patch of wildflowers to greedily sip more nectar as she watched the elves have fun. Just then Mateo did a belly flop into the pond. Ozette laughed, but it came out as a little squeaking noise that no one heard but her.

Next she flew to where she had planted the golden acorn, making sure the ground around the tiny sprout was still moist.

She squinted at the sun and sighed happily as she figured that she still had some time to enjoy before she returned back to her squirrelly self. Up ahead, she saw a field blanketed with red flowers she didn't recognize and zipped toward it.

Chapter Twelve

A Sticky Situation

Boing! Suddenly Ozette was stopped mid-flight. What had happened?

She tried unsuccessfully to flap her wings. They were stuck. She also felt like her face and eyes were covered with a gauzy veil. She tried to balance herself on her little birdie feet, but could barely move them either.

She was stuck, for sure…but in what?

Suddenly she heard a deep voice from behind. "A hummingbird, how delicious! Shall we eat it here or save it for the Spring Fling?"

Alarmed, she wiggled her head around until she found a small hole in the gauze to peek out of. And then almost wished she hadn't as she found herself eye-to-eye with two of the biggest, hairiest, black spiders she had ever seen. She'd gotten caught in a spider's web! She gulped. She had never heard of spiders eating a hummingbird, but there was a first time for everything.

She tried to open her beak to speak, but it was stuck in the web. Slowly, ever so slowly, she managed to pry open her beak enough to say, "Please don't eat me. I'm not really a hummingbird, I'm a – "

"Hear that, Gertie! It says it isn't a hummingbird. It must think we spiders have webs for brains. I know a hummingbird when I see one, and I see one now!" she said.

Ozette drew in a breath, terrified.

"Abigail, the poor thing is scared enough without you taunting her," said the other spider, coming closer to Ozette. "Don't worry dear, we don't eat hummingbirds. Although they might be tasty come to think of it. Just be glad we aren't praying mantises. Yes, indeedy. Be mighty glad."

"I'm Gertie," she said putting two of her eight arms on what Ozette guessed would be her hips.

"I'm Ozette, and I'm really a white squirrel."

The spiders laughed hysterically. This made the web vibrate so violently, Ozette thought she might become ill.

"Oh. A delusional hummingbird. It thinks it's the squirrel who will be our queen," said Abigail, making a fake crown with two of her arms and twirling around.

They chuckled some more, making Ozette feel even punier.

"It's true. I took one of Oliver the elf's magic potions, and it transformed me into a hummingbird for just a few hours. If I stay here much longer, I'll turn back into a squirrel. You'll see. But I'll probably starve to death before that."

Truthfully, Ozette was becoming more and more anxious the longer she was trapped in the web. How could she convince them she really was a squirrel?

Perhaps flattery would get her out of this, er, sticky situation.

"Do you know the talented spiders who wove the web that Baby Fiona the squirrel used for her parachute? It was beautifully crafted. Why, it was the finest parachute I've ever seen," Ozette said, not mentioning it was the only parachute she had ever seen.

"Sure, that would be my Cousin Spinnette and my Aunt Webina," said Gertie. "You've seen the parachute?"

"Baby Fiona, who also is a *squirrel*, is a good friend of mine," Ozette said, emphasizing the word squirrel. "She showed it to me and even let me skydive with it. It's true!" she said, seeing their skepticism.

"Well, I think folks ought to be content being exactly what they were created to be. A skydiving squirrel. Just how foolish is that?" Gertie said, poking the hummingbird's beak with one of her legs.

Suddenly, Ozette felt strange. Her beak was tingling, and her wings were twittering. Her little birdie feet felt heavy. "Oh oh," she squeaked, as she watched her hummingbird body slowly morph back into a squirrel.

Gertie and Abigail looked on in horror, their beady spider eyes growing huge as saucers, as they watched their web slowly torn apart by this white creature that was gradually emerging.

Gertie put four of her legs over her eyes and fainted. Abigail screamed and bolted as fast as her eight legs could carry her away from the web.

"A monster! Monster! Run for your lives!" Abigail shrieked.

Revived by her friend's shouts, Gertie jumped up and took off without a backward glance. Ozette couldn't suppress a giggle as she emerged from the web, once again a squirrel. She was laughing and chortling all the way back to her nest, where she found Oliver waiting.

He rubbed his eyes when he saw her. "I think I need glasses, or maybe I need to lay off the potions. I thought I saw two spiders tearing through the woods, screaming!"

Ozette laughed so hard she rolled on the ground, unable to stop her chuckles.

Oliver approached her tentatively and plucked bits of spider web from her twitching tail and whiskers. "Ozette?" he asked.

She quit laughing long enough to sputter, "Don't ask, Oliver. Just don't ask."

Chapter Thirteen

OLIVER'S MISADVENTURE

Back in her cozy nest, Ozette was deep asleep and dreaming she was being chased by angry spiders. Her legs were pumping as fast as they could but the spiders kept gaining on her. She was startled from her sleep by a frantic voice, shouting, "Ozzzeeette!"

Ozette opened one eye, then the other, yawned and peeked out of her nest cavity.

Sydney, hair disheveled and wringing her dainty fairy hands, was at the base of her tree.

"Have you seen Oliver?" she asked worriedly.

Ozette bolted down the tree, shaking her head. "Not since yesterday," she said, remembering she had last left Oliver when she was doubled over with laughter at the scared spiders.

"We were supposed to go swimming this morning, but he never showed up," Sydney said, biting her lower lip.

"Have you checked his cottage?" Ozette asked.

Sydney nodded. "He's not there. He was at my house until sunset. I gave him some colorful stones to take home for the wall he wants to build. They weren't there either. I'm afraid he never made it home last night!"

Ozette patted the distraught fairy on her back. "We'll find him, Sydney. He probably just stayed with a friend and isn't home yet. You know how Oliver gets when he starts talking."

The two friends started down the path, calling for Oliver. They passed a dragon, two koala bears and a meerkat, but none of the creatures had seen the elf.

"Let's check his cottage again. Maybe he came home while we were searching," Ozette suggested.

When they reached Oliver's cottage, it looked deserted and forlorn. No fire was burning in the massive fireplace and no smell of cooking permeated the air.

"Oliver!" they called in unison, but there was no answer. Ozette briefly wondered if Oliver might have taken the cardinal potion and was flitting around eating birdseed, but then saw the vial still on the table and untouched.

All morning the fairy and squirrel combed the woods looking for their friend. Alerted by their calls, Cassady left Princess Abrianna's cottage and ran as fast as her doggy legs could carry her to where Ozette and Sydney were searching. By noon, the trio was tired and discouraged.

"Maybe Cassady could find him if she has something with his scent on it," Ozette suggested.

"Good idea, Ozette. Cassady and I will run back to Oliver's cottage and see what we can find," Sydney said.

"And I will call for reinforcements," Ozette shouted, as she climbed to the top of an oak tree, flagging her tail vigorously and calling to spread the word that Oliver was missing. Almost instantly, friends of the popular elf joined the search.

Soon Sydney returned with Cassady, who had a pair of Oliver's tiny boxer shorts in her mouth. Oliver was proud of his collection of handmade, miniature boxer shorts that he had even labeled as Oliver Originals. This pair was jet-black with golden embroidered kangaroos.

"I hope Cassady can find his scent. I'm so worried," Sydney said, a tear rolling down her cheek.

They heard a rustling in the trees, and Ozette's squirrel friends Rowdy and Daphne scampered down to give Ozette a sympathetic hug and join the search. Minutes later, her fairy and elf friends Annika, Mateo and Ariel arrived, looking determined and carrying picnic baskets filled with food to give strength to the search party. Everyone picked at the delicious fare politely, but they were all anxious to get back to the search.

They could hear other elves, fairies and animals throughout the forest, all calling for Oliver. With each passing minute, Ozette was becoming more afraid for her friend. Just then she saw McDougal, the nosy magpie, perched on a low branch of a hickory tree.

"Ozette," the magpie called. "Do you know that Oliver is missing?"

"We've been looking all day," she said, nodding.

"I saw him last night!" McDougal said. "He was heading toward home when he suddenly veered off into the forest. I tell you, Ozette. I don't feel good about this. Not good at all," he chattered nervously. "I was going to call out to him, but some weird feeling made me keep my beak clamped shut."

This was even more worrisome. Ozette knew this was a major accomplishment for a magpie since they often talked before they thought.

McDougal ruffled his feathers and tilted his head.

"Lead the way and show us where you saw him," Ozette said.

The forlorn band headed out once again, following the flight path of the black bird.

McDougal led them to the willow grove. Ozette sniffed the calm spring air and wrinkled her nose. What was that awful smell?

Suddenly, Ariel called out from underneath a large weeping willow tree. "Here's the bag of stones! Oliver was here!"

McDougal flew over the area while the others searched the ground relentlessly. A confused Cassady was running in circles, still carrying Oliver's boxers but no longer able to smell Oliver's scent due to the overpowering stench.

Ozette was heartsick. "I may never see Oliver again. Never taste his baking, see his beautiful smile, or go rafting with him," Ozette sobbed, her tears falling onto Ariel's wings.

Ozette sniffed again. The strange smell seemed stronger now. Phew!

"What is THAT?" she cried out, standing on her tiptoes and pointing a paw at a flock of blue jays slowly descending to the ground.

She squinted. They were carrying something. As the flock flew lower, the acrid smell grew. Ozette pinched her nose shut as her eyes grew wide in disbelief! The blue jays had tiny clothespins on their beaks to block the smell! And what was that they were carrying?

She gasped. Whatever it was, it was wearing a pair of blue-and-white-striped boxer shorts. She strained to get a closer look. As the birds drifted to the ground, the smell intensified. The circle of friends drew back, but Ozette stepped closer for a better look. Her furry jaw dropped open in disbelief as the blue jays gently lowered a very dirty, disheveled and familiar-looking elf to the ground.

"Oliver!" Ozette cried.

"Ozette!" Oliver called, holding his arms out for a hug.

Ozette backed up as a wave of the horrible smell wafted closer to her. "You stay right there, Oliver. You smell like a cross between an underground sewer and a rotting swamp," Ozette said, wrinkling her nose. "With maybe some wet groundhog mixed in."

Oliver looked hurt, so Ozette added, "We'll move upwind and you can tell us what happened. We've been so worried!"

"Well, I was walking home from Sydney's when I saw something unusual dart across the road. And you know how adventurous I am," he said, proudly sticking out his elfin chest. "I just had to find out what it was."

The no-nonsense Ariel rolled her eyes. "Foolhardy is more like it," she muttered.

"It was furry and white," Oliver said, ignoring Ariel. "I thought it might be another white squirrel, and I wanted to surprise you with a new friend for the Spring Fling. I was running after it when I fell down into a hole," Oliver said, shuddering.

Ozette clicked her tongue in sympathy.

"And that's how I found out it wasn't a cute white squirrel," Oliver continued. "It was an albino skunk and I had fallen smack down into its lair! He ran out the other side, but not before giving me a good spray in return for his troubles. My tunic was drenched, so I threw it away. By the way, if you didn't know this fact, albino skunk spray smells about a hundred times worse than regular skunk spray."

Ozette nodded in agreement and waved her paw in front of her face to dissipate the odor.

"Then I took a wrong turn in its tunnel and got stuck. I yelled for hours, but no one came. Except the skunk, to give me one final spray," Oliver said, wiping a tear from his eye with the back of a grimy hand and sniffing miserably.

"Tell us how you escaped," Ariel said, impatiently. She was happy Oliver was back, but miffed about the worry he had caused. And besides, she didn't know if this smell would ever wash out of her wings.

Oliver pointed to the small flock of blue jays pecking the ground. "Thankfully, these kind birds heard me. They wove some branches together, put them down into the hole for me to grab, and pulled me out using their beaks," Oliver said. "If they hadn't..." Oliver shivered, unable to continue.

"Now, now, young elf," one of the jays chirped. Blue jays were always optimistic and didn't like to dwell on the negative. "We're just glad we came along when we did. You were in bad shape."

"That elf has quite a set of lungs on him," a second blue jay chimed in. "He was bellowing something fierce, so it was easy to find him. It just took a bit of teamwork to get him out."

"Yes, no problem at all. Glad to help. It's all in

the line of duty," added a third blue jay.

Ozette bowed to the jays and thanked them profusely. She invited them to her home to feast on as much of her stash of seed as their little bellies could hold.

Oliver's tears dried and he smiled weakly. "Good idea. I'm famished!"

"You," Ozette said, "are going straight to the pond for a bath."

Ariel grimaced. "I don't think that's a good idea," she protested. "We drink from that pond."

"Good point," Ozette said. "Let's see if Princess Abrianna can help us."

Oliver sighed as they waved good-bye to the blue jays and headed off for help.

It had started sprinkling by the time the group reached the princess's cottage. But instead of washing the skunk stink away, the rain only intensified it, so Ozette had to stay far upwind from her elf friend.

The princess was in her garden picking flowers and smiled as she saw Oliver and his friends approach. However, once she caught a whiff of the smell, her smile faltered and she began backing away.

"Please, Princess Abrianna," Oliver said, his lower lip quivering. "I got sprayed by an albino skunk, and...well, I've had a terrible experience," he said, too tired to explain the entire embarrassing episode again. "Do you have some herbal potion that will remove this smell?"

"Hmmm," the princess said as she pinched her nose shut with one hand and thought deeply. She raised a finger, saying, "Perhaps. Let me see what I can do."

Oliver started to follow the princess, but she wrinkled her nose and raised her hand to stop him mid-step.

"I'm sorry, Oliver, but you really do smell awful. There are some bumbleberry tarts and garbanzo legumettes in that basket over there, young elf. Help yourself while I mix up something."

Oliver started stuffing food into his mouth as fast as he could. Now if only the princess could remove this skunk stink, he would once again be a happy elf.

Princess Abrianna returned shortly with her hands empty and shaking her head. "I'm sorry, Oliver, but I only have my Regular-Strength Stink-Away Tincture. It works on regular skunk stink, but I don't think it would touch what you got into."

Oliver hung his head. This wasn't his fault. He was just trying to help Ozette. Now there was no way he could go to the Spring Fling smelling like this.

Just then Barnaby came flying up the path as fast as his wings could carry him, with Cassady racing close behind. They were both out of breath, and the elf was clutching a piece of paper in his hand.

"I think I know what we can do for Oliver," he called. "This is my Great Great Granny's special formula. When I heard about Oliver, I dug it out of an old recipe book she gave me."

Ozette took the paper. It was a deskunking mixture of tomato juice, soapwort and essential oil of sage. She shook her head. "I don't think this is strong enough, Bar– "

The princess interrupted her. "Wait! If we add this to my Regular-Strength Stink-Away Tincture, together they might work."

Oliver was excited, but a bit nervous. "Just what's in that Regular-Strength Stink-Away Tincture?" he asked, thinking of some of the exotic ingredients in his potions.

"Oh, this and that. Tansy, spearmint, motherwort, skullcap, agrimony, mistletoe, goldenrod and honeysuckle. You know, the usual. I'll also add some of these blue stones here," she said, pulling four turquoise stones from her pocket. "They will magnify the vibrations of the mixture and increase its potency. I'll mix it all together and stir the concoction counter-clockwise for a bit."

"But where can we get tomato juice in Farlandia?" Ozette said. "It's too early for ripe tomatoes."

The princess smiled. "I've a pantry full of whole tomatoes I canned last summer. And soapwort. Let's not forget that. I had a bumper crop last year," the princess said.

"How will we get juice from these tomatoes?" Oliver asked.

Ozette scrunched up her squirrelly nose and said, "This will be messy, but we can put the tomatoes into a washtub, then stomp up and down on them with our feet, until they turn to juice."

The princess clapped happily. "Perfect! And I'll make a strong soapwort tea and strain it, so you aren't picking bits of leaves out of your hair for a week," she said to Oliver. "Then we'll add the soapy tea, sage oil and the herbal tincture to the juiced tomatoes. Oliver can jump in and soak until he smells better."

Everyone nodded, anxious to help.

The princess grabbed an old washtub, holding her nose as she got near Oliver. She gave him an apologetic look and he grinned sheepishly.

They dumped jars of tomatoes into the tub.

"I'll get the ingredients stirred together while you smash the tomatoes," she said, going inside.

The trouble started with the fairies getting a little too playful. Ariel pitched a ripe tomato at Sydney and hit her in the face, splattering tomato down her chin. Sydney retaliated and accidentally hit Ozette on the back, covering her beautiful white fur with red tomato goo. Even Cassady got into the act, running to and fro, slapping everyone with her tomato-covered tail and happily licking tomato bits off of her friends.

The tomato throwing continued for several more rounds until everyone was covered in bits and dripping red juice.

"Helllllooo?" yelled Oliver finally, from his perch downwind. "I want to get this stink off of me, so quit playing and get to work. Smash those tomatoes, don't wear them!"

The chastised friends laughed and returned to stomping, mashing and smashing until there was nothing left but pulp.

As they stopped to rest, they looked at each other and burst out in giggles again. Now everyone was *covered* from head to toe with red froth!

Just then, the princess came outside with the rest of the concoction. She raised her eyebrows and shook her head, then added her mixture to the juiced tomatoes.

She turned around and gave Oliver the thumbs up, and he dove straight into the tub, tattered boxer shorts and all.

"I hope this works," Ariel muttered, wrinkling her nose.

While Oliver bathed in the mixture, his tomato-covered friends dove into the princess's pond and scrubbed and scrubbed to get the tomatoes off of their bodies and fur. Cassady dove underwater to rinse out a particularly large clump stuck behind her right ear.

Ozette grabbed some soapwort and scrubbed, wondering if she was scrubbing the fur right off of her squirrelly body. Then she climbed onto the bank and shook herself.

Meanwhile, Oliver washed his hair, his little elfin body and even his torn boxers. He lifted his arms and sniffed his armpits.

"Not bad, even if I do say so myself," he said to himself. He scrubbed some more, just to be sure, then ran down the path as his friends climbed out of the pond. Oliver waved and dove into the pond for a final rinse. He looked no worse for wear, although his boxers were torn beyond repair from scrambling through the underground tunnel.

When his friends saw him, they approached cautiously, sniffing the air.

Ozette grinned. She hugged Oliver and he rewarded her with his brilliant smile, happy to be acceptable again.

Princess Abrianna invited her guests to a garden party, where they dined on toadstool tarts and lemon snappers.

After they had eaten, Oliver winked at Ariel. "Don't tell Ozette," he whispered, "but her fur has a decidedly pink cast."

As the motley group bid the princess farewell, Oliver grabbed her hands and thanked her profusely for "de-stinking" him.

"That was some potent potion," he quipped.

"My pleasure, Oliver. Now I have a new formula if this ever happens again," the princess said with a wink.

Oliver shuddered and waved good-bye.

Chapter Fourteen

A Pink Blob Indeed!

T hey were in good spirits, until Baby
Fiona scrambled down a tree onto the
path leading home.

"Is that you, Ozette?" she asked, looking
puzzled at the animal on the trail.

"Of course, it's me. Who did you think it
was?" Ozette asked.

"Well, this may be rude of me to ask, but
why is your fur pink?"

Ozette's squirrelly eyes widened and she

ran to a pond just off the path. Her friends heard a loud shriek as Ozette saw herself reflected in the pond.

"Oh no! My fur is ruined! I'll never look like me again!"

"Oh, come on, Ozette," Ariel chastened her. "You're just a little pink. It's a nice color on you. Brings out your dark eyes."

The truth was, Ozette was a lovely shade of pink, but pink she was.

"I feel like a pink stuffed animal toy," she muttered, as she sat down under a hickory tree.

The friends gathered around Ozette and broke out some dried-fruit snacks to cheer her up. However, their chatter inadvertently disturbed a number of birds napping nearby.

One of the birds, a large white owl, swooped down to the ground. "Ozette," the snowy owl nodded in greeting.

"You recognize me!" Ozette said, relaxing for the first time since she'd seen her reflection.

The wise owl was a tactful bird, but also didn't want to tell fibs. "You're known by the company you keep," he said sagely.

Ozette and her friends were pondering that bit of wisdom that was both literal and figurative when Melanie, a large black magpie, swooped down and tried to grab a tuft of fur off of Ozette's rump.

"Ouch!" Ozette looked up, shocked.

"Oops, sorry," the magpie said, looking baffled. "I thought you were a blob of cotton candy."

Ozette lowered her head, her pink chin quivering. A fat tear rolled down her cheek. Then another. Faster and faster they fell. She cried so hard, a small creek formed on the ground below. Her friends watched in amazement as a flotilla of mice floated down the little creek on leaves, using twigs as oars.

"Oh, no," Ariel muttered. She glared at the magpie, a creature known for blundering insensitivity, and hissed, "You've really stuck your foot in your beak this time."

Oliver shook his fist at the thoughtless bird silently behind Ozette's back.

The magpie slowly began to realize that she had better make amends.

"Blob! Did I say blob?" she chattered nervously. "What I meant to say was a puff – or a poof. That's it – a small poof of lovely cotton candy." She looked hopefully at Ozette and her friends to see if she had fixed her faux pas, but they just shook their heads.

Ozette had had enough. To everyone's

surprise, she suddenly scrambled up a tree and headed back to her nest, flitting from tree to tree as fast as her little pink legs could carry her, muttering to herself as she went. "Pink blob, indeed."

She was unaware that Cassady was trotting along below, keeping a watchful eye on the distraught squirrel as she scrambled along the forest canopy. Ozette stopped to rest on the branch of her favorite hickory tree and looked over her squirrelly body. She surely was not a blob! When Ozette arrived home, she dove into her nest. Cassady lay down under the tree, resting her head on her paws and keeping watch over her upset friend.

Suddenly, something hard rained down on the big dog's head. She sniffed and smelled jumbledberry scones. Cassady looked up quizzically and saw Ozette leaning out of her nest, throwing what appeared to be her entire food stash down to the ground below. Out went half of a neener-neener supreme, some walnutto wafers and her store of pecanettes that Oliver had baked. Cassady snarfed down every morsel, feeling only a little guilty.

"Pink blob, harrumph!" Ozette muttered. "I'll show them. I won't come out of my nest until I'm thin as a twig." Ozette stuffed leaves into her doorway so no one would disturb her and, ignoring her growling stomach, fell asleep.

She woke early the next morning to the sound of whispering outside her nest. She tossed aside the leaves and stuck out her head to find four of her best squirrel-girl friends – Daphne, Zoe, Luna and Nissa – perched on her branch.

"Go away. I'm staying in my nest until I'm not a pink blob," she said crossly.

Daphne held out her paw kindly. "Come with us, Ozette." Ozette shook her head. Daphne grabbed Ozette's paw and pulled her out of her nest. "This is important and will just take a minute."

Ozette reluctantly climbed down her tree with the squirrels, who then led her to a pond.

"Look at us, Ozette," Daphne ordered.

Ozette looked at the four squirrels and shrugged her shoulders.

"Are we blobs?" Zoe asked.

"Of course not. You've normal squirrelly shapes, with lots of muscle from climbing. You look great," she said.

"Look in the pond, Ozette," Luna ordered.

Ozette stared at her reflection. "So what?" Ozette asked, noticing she was still pink.

"Look at your shape, Ozette," Daphne said. "Compare it with ours."

Ozette peered into the pond. She bit her lip. "Why, I look the same size as you! In fact, I'm thinner than you, Daphne," she exclaimed. "I just overreacted at the magpie's words, but realize now that she didn't mean to be hurtful. All of us squirrels need a little extra cushion and muscle, and you are right...we all look just fine! OK, so I'm not a blob. But I *am* definitely pink!" she sighed. "I can't go to the Spring Fling pink! We'll just have to call it off," she said sadly, wondering how canceling her coronation would affect her destiny.

"No way, Ozette," Luna said determinedly. "We're looking forward to your coronation. Besides, we want you to be our queen because of who you are on the inside, not the color of your fur or your shape."

They bid farewell to Ozette, who started home in a much better mood. When she reached her tree, Ozette saw a bespectacled black magpie perched on a limb.

"Hi Ozette. Do you recognize me?" she chirped.

Ozette pursed her lips and cocked her head. There was something vaguely familiar about her visitor, although she had never seen a bird with glasses before.

"I wanted to come by and formally introduce

myself since we didn't have the greatest start," the bird said, politely. "I'm Melanie Magpie. My family has been begging me for months to get spectacles. After thoughtlessly mistaking you for a pink, um, blob of cotton candy, I decided they were right and I got a pair. Now I can see you clearly. And what a lovely pink squirrel you are!"

"Thank you, Melanie," Ozette said, bowing graciously. After all, she still had the same forgiving heart underneath her new pink fur. "Please do come to the Spring Fling, if I still decide to have it."

Melanie's beak snapped open in surprise. "If? If? You must have the Spring Fling. We're all counting on it."

Just then, Ariel landed on Ozette's tree, fluttering her violet wings excitedly. She looked quite pleased with herself and eager to share news.

"I think I found a solution. After you took off, I flew back to Princess Abrianna's cottage. She thinks she can concoct an herbal tincture that will not only make your fur white again, but will also condition it, make it soft and a bunch of other stuff. She's never done it before, but she said it might work. She wants you to come over in the morning."

Ozette agreed, although reluctantly. She had

a lot of faith in Princess Abrianna's abilities, but it was the "bunch of other stuff" that had her worried. While she didn't want pink fur, a big unknown didn't necessarily sound promising either.

Ozette slept late the next morning. She didn't know if it was the quincette quiche or the pearly peachettes that Oliver had brought her, but something had given her nightmares all night long.

She shuddered as she remembered her first dream in which her fur had turned white but then fallen out in large clumps, leaving her bald as a newborn squirrel! In her second dream, her fur started growing, growing, growing, until she looked like a fluffy white mop.

She shook off her dreams and slipped out of her nest. Scampering down the tree, she found Ariel munching on a bunch of grapes and spitting seeds in a most unladylike manner.

"All set to head to Princess Abrianna's to get bleached?" Ariel asked.

"I don't know, Ariel," Ozette said, scrunching up her eyes. "Maybe I'll just let the color fade naturally. We can postpone the Spring Fling until I'm back to normal," she said nervously as she started grooming her pink tail with her claws.

"You can't do that! We always have the Spring Fling in the spring, not three months from now when your fur has grown out! Besides, then we'd have to call it *Summer* Fling, and that doesn't even rhyme! It would have to be the Summer Bummer," Ariel squawked. She grabbed a handful of Ozette's fur. "Plus, unless you want a major fur cut, you're going to look pretty weird as this pink grows out. Have you ever seen a two-toned squirrel?" Ariel shook her head. "I don't think so!"

Convinced but reluctant, Ozette headed to Princess Abrianna's. On the way, she and Ariel ran into several more girlfriends. The beautiful fairy Sydney and the "squirrel-girls" Daphne, Zoe and Baby Fiona gave Ozette an encouraging group hug, and Annika cheered from overhead, her pale green wings shining in the dew-drenched sunlight.

"We came to give you moral support," Annika said.

A few minutes later, they heard Mateo and Oliver call out.

"News sure travels fast in the Farlandia News Network," Ozette said, sighing.

Ozette was touched that friends wanted to join her, but a little wary, too. What if this was a disaster, and she had to hide out for weeks, months even, until her fur grew back to normal?

As if she could read her mind, the ever-cheerful

Annika grabbed Ozette's paw and said, "Keep a positive attitude, dear friend."

The entourage arrived at Princess Abrianna's garden in record time. Ozette was so nervous she almost hoped the princess wouldn't be home. But there she was, outside by her gazebo, stirring a large black pot.

"Hi there! I'm calling this my Super-Duper Pelt-Melt Tincture," she said as she stirred the mixture vigorously.

Pelt-*melt?* Ozette didn't like the sound of that one bit, and she backed away quickly.

The princess smiled and said, "It won't melt away your fur, Ozette, just the pink color." She gave her a wink, "At least, that's my hope."

Ozette looked into the pot and sniffed. It smelled herby, but not unpleasant.

The princess tossed a large amethyst and two smaller pink crystals into the pot. Ozette looked at her curiously.

"Not to worry, Ozette. The vibrations of this mixture should help lift that pink right off your coat.

"Now, hop into the tub," she ordered.

Ozette gingerly entered the tub. The mixture was pleasantly warm and relaxing. She held her breath and ducked under the water, using her paws to scrub her head.

"Maybe this stuff will even remove the gray splotch on your head and that little gray stripe down your back," Ariel said.

Ozette bristled. "Those are an essential part of who I am," she said crossly.

Ariel patted Ozette on the head. "I'm just teasing. Lighten up!" she said.

"Yes, that's what we're hoping for, Ariel," the princess said with a laugh as she added two more pink crystals to the tub.

Minutes later, Ariel shouted, "It's working, Ozette!" The pink color was slowly lightening.

The last step was washing Ozette's fur with a special conditioner made from unicorn milk. The princess massaged the pearly mixture into Ozette's fur then gave her a final rinse.

Finally, Princess Abrianna helped the wet squirrel out of the tub and stood back while she shook herself dry.

"Look at you! Wow!" Ariel said.

Everyone stared at Ozette. Her fur was shiny and beautiful. Best of all, she was white again.

"This calls for a celebration!" the princess said with a grin. "Zoe, Baby Fiona, come help me, please."

A few minutes later, they returned carrying

a pitcher of minty lemonade, a platter of cookies and a large white cake.

"Oliver and Ozette," the princess called as the trio set the treats on a bench in the garden. "As our two adventurers, come serve yourselves first."

Ozette and Oliver walked over to the spread and started laughing. The cake was in the shape of an albino skunk, while the cookies were pink-frosted squirrels.

Oliver started to cut a piece of cake while she munched on a cookie, but Ozette steered his hand with her paw. "No, Oliver. The tail end is for you," she said, winking.

Chapter Fifteen

The Floured Apron Caper

The next morning, Ozette headed down her tree as the dazzling sun began its daily journey across Farlandia. She had just finished planting more nuts when her squirrel-girl friends Daphne, Chloe and Zoe stopped by.

"Princess Abrianna is baking honeyhunkettes for the coronation party and has invited us to help. Come with us!"

As Ozette and her friends jumped from

treetop to treetop, they saw Nissa and Luna and invited them to come along.

"There you are, my squirrely friends," Princess Abrianna greeted them. She pointed at Ozette and said, "There are flowered aprons in a drawer in the kitchen. They should fit and will keep everyone's fur clean."

While the rest of the group went outside to help the princess bring in pots of honey and baskets of pecans, Ozette opened drawer after drawer looking for aprons. Finally, she found a stack of plain pastel aprons.

"Ohhhh," she said, touching a paw to her mouth as she realized these plain aprons weren't the ones the princess had described. Then her eyes lit up. There on the counter was a canister labeled "flour." She opened the lid, carefully filled her paws with flour and meticulously dusted each apron.

"Here are the floured aprons," she called proudly, as the squirrels entered the kitchen followed by the princess.

Princess Abrianna didn't want to hurt Ozette's feelings, so she pretended to have a coughing fit to hide the laughter welling up inside.

"This could be a long day," she whispered, smiling as she gathered ingredients for honeyhunkettes.

Nissa and Luna shelled pecans for the delicacy, while the other squirrels measured, mixed and rolled the other ingredients. They cut the dough into animal shapes, chattering nonstop. Cassady provided cleanup, catching scraps in midair. Princess Abrianna caught Ozette dropping bits of the dough, just so Cassady could have a snack. Ozette grinned sheepishly, when the princess raised one eyebrow at her.

The rest of the baking session went without incident, except when an impatient Zoe chomped on a honeyhunkette before it was cool. But the princess applied an aloe and lavender oil salve to Zoe's sore mouth and she soon felt better.

Ozette curiously peeked into the large pantry while Princess Abrianna rummaged through shelves that were neatly lined with bottles filled with dried herbs, tinctures and salves. Ozette thought it might be helpful, as queen, to know more about healing plants and vowed to ask Princess Abrianna to teach her once the Spring Fling was over.

When they had finished, they sat on the princess's large shady porch in rocking chairs. The chamomile tea, coupled with the rocking motion, was making Ozette sleepy.

Princess Abrianna looked at the group of squirrels in their flour-covered aprons and smiled. "They are dear, innocent creatures," she murmured.

"Well, Ozette, how are the party plans coming? Have you thought about food and invitations?" she asked.

Ozette startled from her dozing. "Well, we're relying on word-of-mouth for invitations," she said.

"And word-of-beak," chimed in Nissa. The princess smiled.

"Oliver invited the eagle that saved us from the creek and his family," Ozette continued. "And Ariel has been flitting all over Farlandia, issuing invitations most efficiently. All of our friends will be there.

"It's a potluck party. Everyone wants to bring their favorite main dish. We're making salads, drinks and desserts," Ozette said, hoping she hadn't forgotten anything. "And no gifts. Not a one do I want," she said firmly.

"It certainly sounds like it's under control. I've lots of vegetables in my garden and will bring salads, honeyhunkettes and root-beer tea," the princess said, slowly rocking in her chair.

Noticing Ozette looking worried and deep in thought, she reached over and patted her paw. "It will be a wonderful party," she said.

Before heading home, the squirrels handed their aprons to the princess. She shook out the flour, still smiling to herself.

When Ozette arrived at her nest, Sydney was there to greet her, hovering above her nest. Sydney's warm smile banished any worries Ozette had about the details of the Spring Fling.

"Oliver has invited us over tomorrow to finish baking for the party and have some lunch," Sydney said, fluttering about. "By the way, have you come up with any games to play at the celebration?" she asked.

Ozette frowned. She had almost forgotten they needed some type of entertainment besides dancing. She would put on her thinking cap and see what came to her.

Chapter Sixteen

WHERE, OH WHERE, HAVE OLIVER'S BOXERS GONE?

The next morning, Ozette, Sydney, Daphne and Ariel gathered in Oliver's super-duper, industrial-strength kitchen to bake up monster batches of chocolate neener-neeners, marshmallow love handles, pecan yummettes and hazelnut-crusted almond smackeroons.

After they had baked dozens of goodies, Oliver served the famished group one of his hallmark lunches: a garden bouquet salad, pistachio pasta with a side dish of ground-acorn surprise, first-flower-of-spring tea and a strawberry pecan parfait for dessert. Not a morsel was left when they were done.

When they finished cleaning the kitchen, Ozette and her friends left amidst giggles and grins. Oliver shook his head, thinking he would never understand silly girls!

Oliver decided to take a shower in his ultra-modern elf bathroom. Wrapped in a towel, Oliver opened his elfin dresser drawer to get fresh boxer shorts. He gasped. Where were his boxers with the fire-breathing dragon design? The boxers with the macaw print that he so loved? His boxers with red squirrels playing pinochle? The giraffe-print boxers? Gone! All gone! Every last one of his designer shorts was gone.

For the next few days, the inhabitants of Farlandia were in a dither as word got out that Oliver's designer label boxer shorts were missing.

Fairies and elves were whispering in disbelief. "Who would do such a thing? How can we find them? We can't check all the elves' boxer shorts; that just isn't proper!"

Poor Oliver was distraught over having to wear plain boring white boxer shorts. That just was not his style. But, loyal friend that he was, he still enthusiastically helped with party plans.

Oddly, whenever Ozette saw him, she grinned a funny smile. It puzzled Oliver, but he shrugged it off as Ozette just being happy about the coming party.

"I'll handle the music and dancing, Ozette," Oliver offered. "Don't worry your furry little head about that."

The party would be held in the woods near Ozette's nest. She consulted Princess Abrianna about the decorations for the surrounding area. Princess Abrianna was touched that the squirrel trusted her to help with this momentous occasion. She suggested that the woods around her nest be filled with flowers and candles that would add a beautiful glow in addition to the thousands of fire-flies that would light up the night sky like stars.

When Ozette whispered in her ear the plan for entertainment, the princess burst into laughter!

The day before the coronation found Ozette sitting deep in thought by the special golden acorn she had planted when she first arrived in Farlandia. A strong, green shoot was slowly growing from the spot, reminding Ozette of how much she, too, had grown during this brief time. The enormity of what she was about to undertake had overcome her during the night, and her inse-curities overwhelmed her as she thought about all that lay ahead. She heard a noise and turned to find Princess Abrianna striding toward her.

"A walnut for your thoughts," the princess said, reaching into her skirt pocket and pulling out a freshly shelled walnut. Ozette shook her head.

"I'm not hungry," she murmured softly.

The princess sat next to Ozette, tucking her sky blue skirt underneath her.

"What's wrong?" she asked. Ozette shook her head, and the princess took her paw in her hand. "Don't tell me nothing is wrong. I can see it in your eyes."

Ozette stared at the ground. "It's just that I don't feel worthy to be queen. Who am I? Just an ordinary squirrel. I know nothing about ruling Farlandia and I have no qualifications. I'm not even very brave. I've never slain a dragon, and I wouldn't even want to."

The princess sighed and held both of Ozette's paws in her hands. "A ruler does not have to be fierce or all-knowing. Think of the qualities you have that will make you a wonderful queen. Look at all that's happened since you found Duchess Zorina. You have proven yourself over and over," she said. She continued, ticking off Ozette's qualities on her fingers. "You are loyal to your friends and are generous and humble. You are clever and creative, loving and kind. Your bravery is not in pitching battles but in doing what is right. Your heart is pure, Ozette. And that is the most important quality of all."

Ozette bit her lip and looked down at the little sprout. She thought of all she had lost, but all she had gained too in her short life, the friendships she had forged and what she had learned from her experiences.

"There's something you don't know. Something I've not told anyone in Farlandia," Ozette said. Tripping over her words with emotion, she haltingly told the princess about her flight from Earth World. "Some of the animals blamed me for the destruction of our beloved home because I'm different," Ozette said, tears springing from her dark eyes. Despite the pain she felt in telling her story, she felt like a great burden had been lifted from her furry shoulders.

"Oh, Ozette," the princess sighed. "How brave you are. Nothing happens by accident. Your journey led you to this place, this time. How can you not see the pattern here? Have faith in yourself, Ozette. The seeds of greatness are in you," she said, tapping Ozette's nose with her finger and looking deeply into Ozette's eyes. Ozette saw such wisdom and, for a fraction of a second, it was like looking into the eyes of her grandmother.

Chapter Seventeen

HAIL QUEEN OZETTE!

Finally the day of the party arrived. Ozette and her friends readied her woods for the celebration. A large banner tied with green ribbons announced, "Hail, Queen Ozette!"

This embarrassed Ozette, but she didn't want to be a bad sport. A small stage had been set up with a hand-lettered sign reading, "The Spice Squirrels in Concert."

Princess Abrianna, followed by an excited Cassady, scurried around seeing to last-minute details.

"Take a nap, Ozette. You want to be fresh for the party," the princess suggested.

Ozette was awakened from her nap by a "Pssst." She peered out of her nest to see the sometimes mischievous Sydney at the base of her tree, holding a basket. "Let's get this set up," she said in a loud whisper. Ozette rubbed her paws together and scrambled down the tree, grinning.

The two headed for a grove of trees just off the main path. They didn't see Daphne hiding behind a bush. As soon as they were out of sight, Daphne scrambled up Ozette's tree and dove into her nest.

That evening, after carefully grooming herself, Ozette stood back and admired her woods. The air was balmy and scented with flowers. Garlands draped the trees, while bouquets in every color imaginable adorned tables stacked high with delicacies. The dragons were carefully lighting hundreds of candles with their flaming breath, while fireflies flitted from tree to tree.

Soon the sky was thick with winged creatures, some carrying animals that lived too far to walk to the party. Fairies and elves flew hand-in-hand, chatting happily. Fairies were dressed in their most colorful attire, and they looked like miniature rainbows as they flitted to the party.

The flowers in their hair added to the heady fragrance of the forest. Elves wore stylish, earth-tone tunics and snug britches and greeted one another with gusto.

Ozette was busy welcoming guests. It seemed that everyone in Farlandia was there. She greeted the eagle who had saved them from the creek and met his family. Everyone from meerkats to minks wanted to congratulate Ozette on her status as queen. Her eyes were starting to glaze over from so many creatures vying for her attention.

Ozette felt a tug on her tail. She turned to find the two spiders, Abigail and Gertie, looking at her sheepishly.

"Thank you for inviting us, even though…" Abigail began.

"Well, that unfortunate incident where…" Gertie said.

Ozette grinned, remembering that day. "Nonsense, I am happy you are here."

"I know you said no gifts, but we wanted you to have this," Abigail said, using four of her legs to hand Ozette a package. Ozette opened it to find yards of beautifully woven spider web. "We dyed it lavender with violet blossoms," Abigail said proudly.

"And Sydney said she'll use it to make a

parachute for you after the coronation," Gertie added.

Ozette was touched. She wasn't sure how one hugged a spider, so she bowed and thanked them for their thoughtful gift, then sent them off to sample a yummy bugette burrito.

Meanwhile, Oliver was running late. He had taken extra time with his hair, grabbed his guitar and now was rushing to the party. As he reached Ozette's woods, his mouth dropped open. His eyes had to be deceiving him. There, hanging from branches of a willow tree, were rows and rows of all of his colorful boxer shorts! And they were filled with creatures bouncing up and down!

Someone had removed the elastic from each waistband, except for about an inch, and flung the circle of elastic over a branch. Each leg hole of the dangling boxers appeared to have been sewn shut, making them look like a line of brilliant little papooses.

Fairies, elves and baby animals were ensconced in the boxers and having a blast jumping up and down. Boing! Boing!

It was a dazzling sight, and Oliver burst out laughing as he realized that his brilliantly colored underwear collection had been made into a bungee jump game!

In his favorite macaw print boxers, Mateo and a baby groundhog were bouncing up and down gleefully and giggling. Annika and Ariel were doubled over with laughter in his red squirrel boxers. Baby sparrows and bee-eater chicks were having a fine time in his fire-breathing dragon boxers, and Bandie, the chipmunk, and Tookie, the cardinal, were climbing into Oliver's giraffe-print boxers for a turn. Two baby bunnies and Milligan Mouse and his extended family waited to join in the fun.

Oliver fell to the ground, howling with laughter! Hearing the commotion, Ozette and Sydney ran over to the elf and hugged him.

"I hope you aren't angry! If you are, it was Ozette's idea!" Sydney said. "And don't worry; you know I can work magic with needle and thread. After the party, your boxers will be as good as new. Well, almost."

"Did you ever think about asking me first?" asked Oliver as he gasped for breath between laughs.

Ozette winked and said, "My grandmother, The Divine Miss Piddlewinks, told me that sometimes it's easier to beg for forgiveness than to ask for permission."

Oliver shook his head in amazement and

hugged them both as shouts of "Whee!" filled the air around them.

The party was in full swing. Several guests had brought instruments and soon the air was filled with music. Birdsong provided a lilting harmony, and cicadas kept a steady beat. Rosie the Ribbiter and her Merry Frog Band's constant "ribbit ribbit" had partygoers tapping their feet.

The Spice Squirrels – also known as Daphne, Nissa, Chloe, Zoe and Luna – mounted the small stage and started singing. Partygoers clapped and swayed to such favorites as "Uptown Squirrel," "Brown-Eyed Squirrel," "Surfer Squirrel," "I've Been Waiting for a Squirrel Like You" and "I Wish They All Could Be Farlandia Squirrels."

When the disco tunes started, Oliver was in his element. Soon, everyone stopped to watch his expert moves. The smooth-moving elf dazzled the crowd as he twirled and executed more and more complex steps. He grabbed Ozette's paw and pulled the embarrassed squirrel onto the dance floor. He soon had her dipping, hip bumping, twirling and pointing a paw at the night sky.

He flashed his brilliant smile and someone whispered, "Wow! He looks just like that disco dude from the Earth World – John Travolta!" Another party-goer quipped, "Yeah. This could be

Saturday Nut Fever."

Ozette and Oliver took a final bow amid claps and shouts of "Encore!"

Chapter Eighteen

THE SECRET OF THE ACORN

M ay I have your attention," said a sweet, melodic voice.

Everyone looked up. A radiant Sydney flew to the center of the stage, her dark hair shot through with the thousands of moonbeams attending the coronation. As if on cue, their old friend Maxwell the unicorn pranced in, carrying Duchess Zorina on his back. Ozette was delighted to see her friend.

Maxwell swooped down and scooped Ozette

onto his back. As he glided under a giant oak tree, Daphne, who was perched on a branch, placed the jeweled tiara on Ozette's head. She had torn Ozette's nest apart that afternoon, finding it.

"Oooh. Ahh," admired the partygoers.

Duchess Zorina patted Ozette's paw with her own and said, "I sneaked out. I couldn't miss this important event. Maxwell will take me back soon."

Princess Abrianna approached the unicorn. She was dressed in forest green, her silver hair crowned with pale yellow lilies. She handed Ozette a beautifully carved piece of wood.

"This is a talking stick. Whenever there are important issues to discuss, pass it to each one, so they can have their say." She glanced at Ariel and whispered in Ozette's ear, "It keeps the gabby ones from doing all the talking."

Ariel opened her mouth to protest, shut it, grinned and wrinkled her nose good-naturedly at Princess Abrianna.

"I now crown you, Queen Ozette of Farlandia," said Princess Abrianna, smiling up at Ozette.

The jubilant crowd cheered and clapped their hands, paws, claws and wings. A bevy of fireflies descended on Ozette, surrounding her with their twinkling lights.

Ozette gulped. She was filled with emotion as she looked out at the joyous crowd, their trusting faces aglow in the candlelight. How quickly they had accepted this lone white squirrel into their family. Ozette vowed she would be the best queen Farlandia had ever had, forgetting she was also the first Queen of Farlandia so hopefully that wouldn't be too difficult.

The party continued into the night. Ozette sang, danced and visited. She was so busy she hardly had time to sample the scrumptious array of foods. Finally, she managed to steal away for a few minutes to visit with Duchess Zorina.

"You look lovely," Ozette told the Bichon, who was freshly bathed and groomed and looked like a white powder puff.

Duchess Zorina kissed Ozette's paw. "You're the enchanting one. The tiara looks wonderful on you."

"I hope you didn't get into trouble for giving this to me," Ozette said, fingering the tiara.

"They think I buried it in the garden. Not to worry. They bought me a new one."

They heard a flapping of powerful wings, and Maxwell nodded that it was time to leave. Using his large teeth, he set down on the ground two overflowing baskets of goodies specially made for Ozette by the palace cook. Ozette thanked him and hugged Duchess Zorina, promising they would meet again.

The merrymaking continued long past Ozette's usual bedtime, until every dance was danced, every song was sung and every crumb was eaten. As the party was slowly breaking up, she realized how tired she was. She thanked and hugged the guests. When the last one had said good-bye, she slowly climbed the tree to her nest.

She felt her head for her tiara. How well it fit! Like it had been designed for her. And she loved how beautiful it looked on her head. Perhaps being a queen might be fun, after all.

As she peered out of her nest, the night creatures continued their comforting calls. She curled onto her back and carefully combed her tail with her claws, removing bits of the honeyhunkette that Ariel had accidentally dropped from the branches. She heard the strains of a song the Spice Squirrels were singing in their sweet, clear voices as they wound their way home:

> *"The moon and stars they light our way,*
> *Our path is smooth and clear.*
> *The sun gives warmth upon our woods,*
> *Blessing what we hold dear.*

Tonight our forest sings with joy,
For earth and sky have met.
We have a queen, a lovely queen,
The fairest Queen Ozette."

Ozette smiled drowsily then felt something lick her nose tenderly. She sleepily opened her eyes and saw the shadow of her beloved grandmother, The Divine Miss Piddlewinks, in the moonlight.

"Well done, my child. Well done," her grandmother murmured, and then disappeared into the night.

Ozette awoke late the next morning. She stretched lazily, reliving the events of the past day and realizing she truly was Queen of Farlandia, although she didn't feel any differently than she had before the coronation. Her tiara had fallen rakishly over one ear. She plucked it from her head and gazed at it, then gasped. During the night, the flower at the tip of her tiara had been transformed into a beautiful golden acorn.

Not even stopping to snag a bite of breakfast, she scurried down her tree and scampered to where she had planted the golden acorn. Overnight, the tiny sapling had grown into a sturdy tree, a tree resplendent with pale, golden leaves reaching skyward.

Ozette sat quietly under its branches, thinking about her grandmother and realizing that fulfilling her destiny was an ongoing journey, not an end in itself. As she watched the sunlight filter through its leaves, the tree seemed to glow with an inner light, casting its radiance on the lone white squirrel with a promise of even more adventures to come.

Recipes

O zette and her friends hope you'll enjoy trying some of their favorite recipes. They like to eat healthy foods so that they have plenty of energy for adventuring, rafting, skydiving and other outdoor activities. Feel free to add your own touch to the recipes.

So brew up a cup of mint tea, relax and imagine your Farlandia friends are sitting next to you. Who knows? With all the magic in the air, you might be surprised at what can happen.

*Safety Note: Like those in Farlandia, some of these recipes use real, edible flowers. Please make sure any flowers you use have not been sprayed with chemicals. Also, food processors are wonderful for chopping ingredients quickly, but the blades are very sharp. Have an adult do the chopping or, if you do it, be very careful. If you don't have a food processor, you can hand chop the fruit and nuts and give 1/2 of the oatmeal a quick whirl in a blender.

Garden Bouquet Salad – makes about 6 servings. Ariel loves this salad and has been known to pick all of the violets from it and gobble them down. She swears it makes her violet eyes brighter. You can personalize this salad by adding or subtracting whatever you like. Add a little cheese or nuts for a main dish.

Ingredients

1 package organic Spring Mix (if you grow your own salad greens, that is even better)

Snippets of young dandelion greens (optional) (These can come from your yard – but not if they have been sprayed with chemicals. You can also find these at some larger supermarkets.)

1/2 can of garbanzo beans (chick peas), drained

1/2 cup cherry or grape tomatoes

3 chopped green onions

1 stalk chopped celery

1/2 cup sliced olives – black or green

1 cup broccoli florets

1/2 cup freshly picked unsprayed violets from the woods or garden. Later in the season you can use nasturtium flowers. Yummy.

Mix well in your prettiest salad bowl. Toss with your favorite dressing.

Jumbledberry Scones – Makes 8.

Unless you live where elves and fairies are growing jumbledberries, you may have to make some substitutions. Ozette suggests you use a jumble of dried fruits for the same taste. She likes a mix of dried cranberries, dried blueberries and dried cherries, but feel free to experiment with other combinations.

Ingredients

2 cups flour (Ozette likes organic whole wheat pastry flour for her scones)

2 tablespoons sugar

1/2 teaspoon salt

3 teaspoons baking powder

2 eggs

4 tablespoons butter or margarine

1/3 cup heavy cream or milk

1/2 to 1 cup jumbledberries or dried berries of your choice. How much you use depends on how fruity you want the scones.

1 cup coarsely chopped nuts (Ozette loves walnuts or pecans in these, although you can use any nuts. Use more or less depending on how nutty you like your scones.)

2 teaspoons sugar to sprinkle on top

Mix the flour, 2 tablespoons sugar, salt and baking powder in a bowl. Using a fork, cut in the butter until the mixture looks like fine crumbs. Add the dried berries and nuts. Mix well. Add the eggs and cream to make a stiff dough.

Most recipes call for rolling out scones and cutting them, but squirrels are too impatient for that. Ozette likes to flour her paws (wash them first), divide the dough into 8 pieces, and pat each piece until it is fairly flat but still a little mounded. Sprinkle each round with a little sugar.

Arrange on a greased cookie sheet and bake at 400 degrees F for 15 minutes or until browned. Enjoy with a cup of honeysuckle tea or other beverage.

Nutty Fruitinas – Oliver developed this recipe and loves to add new kinds of nuts and seeds to the cookies for his friends. They freeze well. (The cookies, not his friends.)

Ingredients Group One
3 cups mashed bananas
2 teaspoons ground cinnamon
1/3 cup oil (Ozette likes coconut oil)

Mix well with a spoon.

Ingredients Group Two
Put 1 1/2 - 2 cups of dried fruit in a food processor. Ozette loves a mixture of raisins, dried berries and dried fruits. Her favorite combo is dried cherries, dried cranberries, dried pineapple and dried apricots, but you can experiment.

Then add:
1 1/2 cups old-fashioned oats (uncooked)
2 cups pecans or other nuts
1 cup of seeds (This is optional. Ozette likes to use pumpkin and sunflower seeds.)
These all go into the food processor and are processed until well blended.
Add group two to group one.

Then add 1 1/2 cups uncooked oats to this mixture. Be sure to mix well and spread on two greased cookie sheets. Bake at 315 degrees F for 40-50 min. When cool, cut into squares.

Chocolate Neener-Neeners

Ingredients
2 cups mashed ripe bananas
1/2– 2/3 cups dark chocolate powder
1 cup dried fruit (cranberries, blueberries and/or cherries are especially good)
1 cup walnuts or pecans
1/2 cup unsweetened coconut
1 cup semi-sweet chocolate chips
2 cups uncooked old-fashioned oats, divided

**To turn these into chocolate neener-neener supremes, increase to 2 cups of semi-sweet chocolate chips.

Put the nuts, fruit and 1/2 of the oatmeal in a food processor. Process until chopped and mixed.

Put all ingredients into a mixing bowl. Using a spatula or wooden spoon, mix until well blended.

Grease a cookie sheet and evenly spread the mixture on the sheet. Bake at 350 degrees F for

30-35 minutes, depending on how moist you want them. Cut into squares.

Spinach Quichette – serves 4

Ingredients
1 pound fresh spinach steamed for 10 minutes
2 shallots
2 cloves of garlic, peeled
Salt and pepper to taste
1 teaspoon oil to coat the pan
7 ounces goat cheese (if you don't like goat cheese, mozzarella or feta are also good)
5 large eggs (Ozette likes free-range organic eggs)
2 ounces sun dried tomatoes (optional)

If using a food processor, process shallots and garlic in a food processor until minced. Otherwise hand-chop them. Add cheese and eggs and puree until smooth. You can use a food processor or a blender.

Oil an 8x8-inch baking pan. Spread the lightly steamed spinach on the bottom of the baking pan. Pour egg mixture over spinach and bake at 425-degrees F for 20 minutes, or until the top is browned and a table knife inserted in the center of quiche comes out clean.

*This is also good using lightly steamed asparagus and sautéed mushrooms. Buy mushrooms at the grocery store - don't gather mushrooms from the wild. Ozette can eat mushrooms that could be poisonous to her human friends, so buy yours at a human store!

Lemonette Linguini serves 4-6

Ingredients

1 pound linguini (Ozette likes whole wheat for the fiber)

juice from 2-3 lemons, depending on how lemony you want it

zest from 1 lemon

1/3 cup chopped fresh parsley

1/2 cup chopped green onions

1/2 cup extra virgin olive oil

Salt and pepper to taste

1/2 – 2/3 cup chopped nuts (Ozette likes this with pistachios or pecans)

1/2-1 cup grated Parmesan cheese

Cook pasta according to package directions. Drain in a colander. Toss all of the ingredients in a bowl until well blended. You also can add chopped tomatoes, basil or snow peas if you like.

Pistachio Pasta serves 4-6

Ingredients
1 pound whole wheat angel hair pasta
1 1/4 cups milk
6 ounces feta cheese (If you prefer, you can substitute blue cheese. Ozette wants to try it with mozzarella sometime.)
1 tablespoon butter
1/2 cup shelled pistachios
2 tablespoons fresh, chopped parsley

Cook pasta according to package instructions. Meanwhile, melt the butter in a frying pan and add pistachios. Sauté until nuts are fragrant. Add milk and cheese. Cook over low heat until feta has melted. Drain pasta in a colander. Put pasta in a bowl, add cheese mixture and toss until blended. Sprinkle chopped parsley on top.

Bugette Burrito – serves 4. Our favorite spiders, Abigail and Gertie, insisted that their Bugette Burrito recipe be included. Ozette put on her thinking cap and came up with a variation – minus the bugs – she thinks you will like.

Ingredients

4 9-10-inch flour tortillas

1-2 cloves chopped garlic

3/4 cup chopped onion

2 teaspoons vegetable oil

1/2 teaspoon ground cumin

1/2 teaspoon chili powder

1 cup chopped red bell pepper

1/2 cup frozen corn kernels, thawed

1 2/3 cups canned black beans, rinsed, drained

2 teaspoons minced seeded jalapeño chile (omit if you don't like spicy foods)

2 medium tomatoes, chopped

2 cups lettuce, torn into small pieces

Plain non-fat Greek yogurt

Your favorite salsa

8 tablespoons grated Monterey Jack cheese (about 2 ounces)

4-6 tablespoons fresh cilantro, chopped (omit if you don't like cilantro)

Preheat oven to 350-degrees F. Wrap tortillas in foil. Warm in oven until heated through, about 15 minutes.

Meanwhile, heat oil in a large skillet. Add garlic and onion. Stir over medium-high heat until golden, about 4-6 minutes. Add cumin and chili powder; stir. Add bell pepper and corn; sauté until almost tender, about 4-5 minutes. Add beans and jalapeño (if using); Simmer on low heat for 8 minutes. Season with salt and pepper. Remove from heat.

Place warm tortillas on plates. Spoon filling down the center, dividing equally. Top each with 2 tablespoons cheese, then 1-2 tablespoons each of Greek yogurt and cilantro. Add lettuce, tomato, and salsa. Fold sides of tortillas over filling, forming packages. Turn each package, seam side down, onto plate.

Garbanzo Legumettes – Ozette hates getting popcorn kernels stuck in her teeth, so her friends devised this recipe. It's a crunchy, delicious snack that is a wonderful change from popcorn.

Ingredients
3 cups cooked chickpeas (garbanzo beans) or substitute 3 cups of canned chickpeas (about 2 15-ounce cans), rinsed and well drained.

1/4 cup olive oil

6-8 cloves of finely minced garlic – use more or less depending on how well you like garlic. (Ozette claims it helps her stay healthy.)

Salt and pepper to taste, if desired

Preheat oven to 450-degrees Fahrenheit. Using paper towels, pat chickpeas dry. Lightly grease a cookie sheet with cooking oil.

In a large bowl, toss together chickpeas, oil and garlic. Season lightly with salt and pepper if using. Spread in single layer on cookie sheet.

Stir occasionally while baking. Bake 30 to 40 minutes, or until chickpeas are very crunchy but not burned. Cool 5 minutes before serving.

About the author

Originally from Washington state, Judy lives on 17-acres in the mountains of North Carolina with her husband and four rescued dogs. She has worked in environmental education, feature writing, advertising and university teaching. Judy's writing is influenced by her love of nature and work with Bichon Frise rescue and wildlife rehabilitation. When she's not writing, she loves to raise and use herbs, bicycle, hike, camp and visit family on the West Coast. Visit her website at www.talesfromfarlandia.com.

Made in the USA
Charleston, SC
17 July 2013